Smashing Laptops
a Nomad's Romance

JOSH WAGNER

Buckwheat Dreams
Hamilton, Montana

Published by Buckwheat Dreams, Missoula, Montana.

Smashing Laptops is a work of fiction, except for the parts that aren't.

Library of Congress Cataloging-In-Publication Data
Smashing Laptops / Josh Wagner — 4th ed.
Asymmetrical Press, 2015
ISBN: 978-1-68287-016-7
eISBN: 978-1-68287-016-2

1. Fiction. 2. Memoir. 3. American West. 4. Missoula. 5. Jackets.

Chapter Two, Section 0: Albuquerque, NM first appeared as
"Salt of the Earth" in CAFE IRREAL vol. 10, 2003

Chapter Four, Section 5 first appeared as
"Smashing Laptops" the short story in CEDILLA vol. 2, 2008

Zozezaz Diagram by Anthony Gregori
Illustration "Quit Looking Drunk" © 2011 Katie Ludwick (ladypajama)
Illustration "Hello Alien" © 2011 Katie Ludwick (ladypajama)
Photo "Pickaxe and Telephone Wires" © 2011 Rebecca Schaffer

Cover design by Alyssa English
Formatted in beautiful Montana
Printed in the U.S.A.

Buckwheat Dreams

For the Ludwicks

"They have pretty blue flowers over there.
Swarms of little, pretty blue flowers...
I guess they blame those on the Russians, too."

— LISLE MUELLER CHESTNUT (1916 – 2010)

"And if I die in Raleigh at least I will die free."

— KETCH SECOR

Smashing Laptops
a Nomad's Romance

San Francisco, CA

I ONCE KNEW A WOMAN who built her own boyfriend. She lived in some abandoned place in Oakland and her boyfriend lived in one of the empty rooms. I guess you'd call him a sculpture, but she called him boyfriend. We went on a few dates and played board games in her studio, but she always told me as soon as boyfriend was finished, so was I.

She made him out of junk, non-recyclables she found around town and brought home. Torn up tires, twisted old highway signs, rusty wire, bits of styrofoam. His lips were fake coral from a fish tank she found with a "free" sign on it out in front of a fancy house in Pinole. His left eye was a red snooker ball. She hadn't found the right one yet.

We used to hang out in San Francisco with a group of street kids who slept on the Haight. The first time she introduced us, they were all stretched out along the side of a building. Seven in a little row sharing one cigarette. They had a dog, but the dog didn't smoke. I sat next to them while Sculpture Girl held my hand. We all got into a heated discussion about Batman. They explained how they were vigilantes, and it was their job to keep the Haight straight. "Dudes piss on people's doors or mess with girls—we put a stop to it."

None of these kids were a day over 18, so I smiled and listened but didn't think much of it, until a little while later this pair of dreaded-out hippies walked by. One of them tossed a beer bottle. It shattered on the ground. Well, these street kids were up in a flash and a second later they formed a tight little circle around the hippies. I thought there'd be a fight, but one vigilante, all decked out in spiked leather, started calmly explaining to the hippies exactly why breaking bottles on the street was bad for everybody. He said, "Not only is it stupid, but that kind of shit brings the cops. Then they start harassing everyone more and more, and the Haight turns into a bad place to be."

Earlier that week I'd passed two officers talking to an old man snuggled up in a doorway with his sleeping bag. One cop said, "You need to put the pipe away or we'll have to take it." That's how chill this place was. And the street kid was right. Start breaking beer bottles for no good reason, and all that changes.

Anyway, the whole scene ended up with the hippies saying they understood and they were sorry. They cleaned up the broken glass, and Sculpture Girl asked if she could put the pieces in her backpack. "It's for my boyfriend," she said. Then everyone, vigilantes and hippies alike, shared a round of hugs.

It was the most beautiful thing I'd ever seen, and I fell in love with San Francisco.

There is no moment like this by which I define the little city of Missoula, Montana. She is too close. Missoula is not the lover you meet in the rain for a torrid night of passion and never see again. Missoula is the blanket you wrap yourself up in every night until you've nearly forgotten she exists. It's only when you find yourself in bed without her that you realize just how important she was every day of your life.

I remember climbing up to the "M" after a three-day fast, taking mushrooms and looking down on Missoula as if she were a toy city beneath a Christmas tree.

I remember Jays Upstairs, where you could go to a rock show and do your laundry at the same time.

I remember wandering through town under a quiet snowfall after all the power had gone out.

I remember the homeless Salish man who carved a cane for me on the walking bridge. And the white-eyed man who changed my entire night and possibly my entire life by saying, "Don't be afraid," as he walked past me on his way to the river.

I remember getting lost in Missoula long after I

thought I'd walked every street and seen every corner. Losing my bearings in a place so familiar felt no less disorienting than if I'd stumbled around the bend to find a midnight bazaar selling shrunken heads and dried centipedes. Even small towns have enough nooks to last the rest of your life, though you may need a magnifying glass to find them.

I remember Missoula's very own Leprechaun offering business card wishes from behind his beard. *Fantasmagorical*!

I remember bowling with wine bottles on the Northside.

I remember the night Levi brought my dog Lucyfurr to me days after I'd decided I wasn't responsible enough to keep her. He said, "The guy who adopted her is a dick, so I kidnapped her and now she's yours." And she was my traveling companion for 8 years.

I remember chasing girls and making up stories. I remember two drunk kids who took us out to the woods and gave a sermon on Bill Burroughs and Louisiana and spewed whisky on the fire and seasoned our visions with charisma until the sky paled and we returned haggard and pathetic to Finnegan's, where we stole postcards and mailed them to random people we found in the phone book.

Which reminds me, I got a postcard from Sculpture Girl a few months after leaving California. On the front was a picture of the bay taken from the Albany Bulb. She told me boyfriend left her for a twenty foot tall wooden statue of a woman made out of driftwood. Said she was moving to Alaska to peel shrimp.

I remember book battles at the Colonel Fun Show, wine-drunk, where me and Dean mashed up sex manuals with cookbooks, and Pynchon with Seuss.

I remember offering french fries to strangers with Bosco, and trading random shit from the drawer for a rubber chicken and a bucket of beer.

I remember the great bee massacree of '93.

I remember falling in love, night after night after night. You women are all so beautiful it makes a guy wonder what he's even doing on this planet.

I have enough memories of Missoula to bore you a thousand times over, but there is no defining moment.

Believe me, I'd tell you if there was.

CHAPTER ONE

KATIE LUDWICK

1.

IT'S EARLY SEPTEMBER, 2:17am. My Greyhound departed from the Las Vegas what seems like a hundred hours ago. We're forty-eight miles outside Missoula, Montana, where we've stopped in the dark shadows of pine trees. Yellow light winces through the fog. My forehead stamped against the cold glass.

Earlier today, the lady at the ticket counter had asked me if I was going home. She had to ask twice before I understood the question.

"I forgot my jacket," is what I told her. I was trying to be funny, but I was actually kind of serious so the joke didn't work. She just stared at me like I was crazy.

Now I'm totally broke. I've never been so broke in my

life. No dollar bills crumpled up in pockets, no quarters floating around my backpack. Not even a blank check to bounce. I try to cram my legs into a comfy position in the impossibly awkward greyhound seat. No one gets off, no one gets on. Lights out. I stare through the dirty window at haggard shapes watching from wood porches and chairs that have been sitting around for decades. I close my eyes and wait for the bus to move again.

I'm going home. Back to Montana. Back where it's safe and quiet. Back where I belong.

I'm kidding myself. I don't belong there, and neither does anyone else.

Only bears and wildflowers belong in Montana.

2.

Took me almost six weeks to escape Vegas. Probably the longest six weeks of my life. Spending a summer in Las Vegas is not something one decides to do. It happens quick and brutal, like a mugging—when your eye is on a woman's ass, your head is in the clouds, and your legs are marching lockstep to the four-letter heartbeat of the single cause and cure for all of mankind's ills. Yeah, okay. I'd fallen in love.

It was 112 degrees and not even August the day I finally decided to get my ass back to Missoula. I'd been sitting all afternoon in a small studio apartment on Tropicana, slumped in front of five fans and a swamp cooler. Together they worked it like a junkyard band as

I through the obstacle of their rhythm. I swore my eternal devotion to Montana's crabby climate, envisioned her lush arteries, and spritzed my face with a green plastic squirt gun.

I could think of nothing better to do in that lonely Las Vegas meltdown than lock myself away from the sun and think about rolling stones and how much harder it was each day to get out of my chair. This wasn't me. This was the lump love left over. I needed to move, but nothing moved me. I don't recommend falling in love in Vegas. When it doesn't work out, the game feels rigged. Thanks for playing. Come back when you've got more to lose! Loss is a religion in Vegas, I don't care if it's money, sanity, or a woman.

Correction: I no longer believe there's any such thing as "losing" a woman. A man loses himself as women slip into the future.

Anyway, there I was, wondering for the millionth time how it had all come down to this, when the phone rang.

It was a wall phone, and I found it hiding under a pile of dirty towels. I could hear my old friend Katie Ludwick breathing on the other end of the line. She did not say hello. Or rather, she did say hello, but she said it like this: "I'm pregnant."

3.

The Katie Ludwick in my mind is six inches taller than the Katie Ludwick of flesh and blood. She wears an iron girdle and a buckler, with a fiery orange skirt sewn from sundry reptilian skins. Her valkyrie white hair cracks like willow branches in the wind. Storm clouds and flash mobs reflect in her eyes. She breaks walnut shells with her teeth, but then spits them out because she hates walnuts. She is always standing on the edge of some cliff.

Photos reveal a different story. In this one, her eyes are calm, delighted. Here she tinkers patiently with a sewing machine. Cross-legged on the floor, she reads the *Outlaw Bible of American Poetry* or clips photos from *National Geographic*. She is five-foot-five inches tall, with shoulder length dishwater blonde hair, wide hips, and a moderate pouch of flab hanging over the lip of her pants. She has a snaggletooth and chapped lips. Freckles. Her eyes are muddy green. After a good cry her cheeks puff up like pomegranates. She likes walnuts but can't eat them because she's allergic.

I've known Katie Ludwick most of my life. She's my best friend's little sister and that sort of makes her my little sister too.

That afternoon on the phone Katie laughed like a lunatic, and I could hear her scratching her briar patch hair into an even bigger briar patch.

"I can't have babies, Josh! I'll make a terrible mother. I don't like to take care of people. I'm not a caring person. I'm not compassionate. I'm selfish. I always want things to go my way."

I could relate.

"Come home," she said.

"I will," I said.

"When?" she said.

"I'm broke," I said.

"I'm broken," she said.

"Pregnant is not broken."

"Something feels broken."

"It's like the opposite of broken."

"Just come home," she said.

"I'll find a way," I said.

"Promise?"

"I'll find a way."

In her entire life, Katie Ludwick has only had one boyfriend. His name is Adam Jostler. They've been living together for a while now, and he is not the father of her child.

Before hanging up the phone, Katie told me how she found out about her condition. She'd only gone to see her doctor on account of stomach problems and lethargy. Plagued by a dozen food allergies, Katie worried over what she would have to give up this time. The doctor told her to sit down. A nurse brought her some water.

The doctor diagnosed no new allergy. Instead she found the tides of nature tumbling, inward instruments turning, tuning to the twist of hidden clocks.

When the doctor told her she was pregnant, all Katie could say was, "Oh."

Stumbling out of the waiting room, she bumped into a table and spilled a jigsaw puzzle onto the floor.

When she was back among friends, Katie endured their coos and congratulations. She dodged questions about the father's identity. Not out of embarrassment, but out of confusion. The father of her new fetus had no identity. This wasn't a case of too many possible lovers to choose from, but of too few.

Our little Katie was a virgin.

4.

The nouveau lights come on and the air-brakes fizzle. I'm awake. The hulking mass of the bus driver's silhouette looms incandescent around the edges.

"Greyhound: We don't give a fuck because you don't give a fuck."

"What?" I say, and my question squeezes through half-glued eyelids.

"I said everyone has to get off here, sir."

The driver parrots his lines with all the enthusiasm of a broken toothpick: "Take your bags, valuables, and belongings with you. Greyhound is not responsible for the loss or theft of any bags, valuables, or belongings."

"Where are we?"

He doesn't answer. He's already miles off down the aisle, rustling up the next passenger.

Every place looks the same through a Greyhound window. I only know I'm in Missoula because I just know.

There's another reason I'm going home besides Katie, and that's to get my jacket. It's one of those 80s faded blue denims with a comfy gray lining. Torn to tatters, covered in safety pins. A thick gray hood and broken cinch strings. I call it a boxer's jacket because my best friend Dean wore it in high school and back then he was a boxer. But maybe it's just the connection making me think it looks like a boxer's jacket. Maybe it doesn't look like a boxer's jacket at all. As far as I know, there isn't even any such thing as a boxer's jacket.

I left the jacket in Montana because Katie said she'd take care of it while I was gone. I can only hope she's too pregnant to wear it or I might never get it back at all. Me and Katie Ludwick, we're both in love with the same jacket.

God, I miss that jacket. I think things in Vegas might have gone down differently if I'd had it with me. I sometimes wonder if my subconscious schemed for all that drama to go down just so I'd have a good excuse to come home. Of course, Katie Ludwick's belly is the main reason for my trip. She's been carrying that fatherless child for eight months now, and I swore an oath I'd be there when she delivers.

All I know now is I need to see Katie Ludwick and I need to get that jacket. That's why you turn around and go back, to get the things you left behind.

5.

Another bus is scheduled to arrive from Seattle. On board is Amelia, the lady I tell my secrets to. Well, most of them anyway. We're like twins from mirror universes. Exactly alike in opposite ways. She worked it all out so we would arrive at the same time: me from the south, her from the west. This was the plan. We'll meet in Missoula on separate greyhounds, she said. Let's not tell anyone we're coming back, she said. No one to meet us at the station but each other, she said. We'll both pretend we're there to pick the other up, it'll be a riot, she said.

When Amelia hugs me and says, *Welcome back to Missoula*, and I say, *How was your trip*, she'll respond with something like, *It hasn't been the same around here since you've been gone*, and I'll give her a comforting, *I'll bet you're tired, I've got the couch all set up for you.*

My bus was supposed to roll in at ten, but Idaho Falls turned out to be a "breakdown stop." Greyhound has pickup stops, meal stops, and breakdown stops.

I couldn't call from the road to tell her I'd be late because I don't have a cell phone and we've reached the technological cusp where I no longer understand pay phones. Logically, I understand them. You put quarters in and the phone decides how long you get to talk. But emotionally, I've lost touch. I can no longer bring myself to use one.

"Oh My God, we broke down too!" She'd only been waiting on me for about a half hour. Her voice is soft, stern, and precise. Like a fourth grade teacher. "This invasion was planned by providence," she said.

Amelia's hair is bright burgundy, freshly dyed. Her cheekbones are high granite cliffs overlooking the alpine lakes inside her eyes. An haute couture jacket way beyond her pay grade buckles over a goodwill tee-shirt and plaid skirt. Black boots to her knees—the heels of a bull.

"You really didn't tell anyone you were coming?" I say.

"That was our plan. Did you tell anyone?"

"Nope."

"Good. Let's call someone. I'm not carrying this big-ass bag all the way down Broadway."

Her bag was indeed big-ass. Army duffle bag packed to the gills. What is it with girls?

"What is it with girls? I thought you were only staying a few days."

"I have… things." She polishes her hands over the bag's canvas surface as if the gesture explained it all.

"Wasn't our plan to walk into town all anonymous?"

"Yeah. Let's not."

From her Hello Kitty purse Amelia produces a pack of American Spirits. She gazes into a pink clamshell make-up mirror to light up, displaying a certain genius in the way she flutters her eyelashes. She chooses her words like a military strategist. Uses cigarettes like wands. Always taps her ashes—never flicks.

"Why not?" I argue. "I've been on the bus twice as long as you, and I'm up for it."

"Yes, because you have no bag," she says.

"We'll stash it somewhere."

"We are not stashing my bag anywhere other than the trunk of the car that comes to pick us up."

Of the local friends between, three have cars. This is just the way Missoula is. You bundle up and ride your bike in the snow and you like it.

Providence, being who she is, made sure no friends with cars would be available to receive our call. We do not wait for the tone and we do not leave a message. Instead, I carry Amelia's bag to the nearest church and we stash it in the bushes.

"You're right, this was a good idea," she says at last. We are free and easy on the quiet street. On beyond, little mountains cradle the low skyline of the city.

"I can't wait to see Katie."

"I know. I bet she's huge."

"Tell me the truth. Do you think Adam is the father?"

"I don't know anymore than you do," I say.

Amelia nods. She sets her gaze down the road. "Katie says she's a virgin. That's good enough for me. No father it is." And then she catches me off guard: "Anyway, I heard they broke up."

Broke up? "Katie and Adam?" I can't believe it.

"It's what I heard," she says.

Katie and Adam are like a staple of love and fidelity and everything's-gonna-be-okay-ness. The news continues to stagger me.

"Let's go down to the river!" Amelia says.

"Right now?"

"Yes. Right now."

"It's too late," I say. "I need sleep."

"You sound old," she says.

"Never!"

"You're like a tall five-year-old."

"The plan has always been to skip middle age and jump straight from youth to crotchety old asshole."

She bites my shoulder and growls. "Tell me what you really want," she says.

This is not a question that makes me comfortable.

"I'll go first," she says. "I want to leave my

fingerprints everywhere. Touch a million hearts. Never satisfied. Always hungry…Now you."

"Fine," I say. "I want to be a relic."

"Explain."

"I want to change the world, but not right away. Not for hundreds of years. I want far off future people to find my stories in a box somewhere. And then I want those stories to inspire some crazy new theory no one ever thought of before. To accidentally influence the genius who finally figures out time travel or realizes cruising through worm holes is actually pretty easy. Or discovers a brand new way of trying to understand God."

"God is in the river," she says.

"We'll go tomorrow."

"That's all I want to do, okay? Just once before I leave. Stand by the river and look at it. Maybe try to break it."

"Break it?"

"Break it."

"Okay…"

"It's not too much to ask."

"No, it isn't."

For now it's enough to see our river in the distance. The Clark Fork claims territory from the city, a canyon of overgrowth climbing up toward this sterile sidewalk that passes for a rocky path. We move upstream almost at a gallop until Amelia's bad knee starts to hurt. We hold hands. The spade of our arms sways between us. It's an overcast night, so we pray for stars.

Amelia, who can drift effortlessly from debutante to relentless bitch to supple kitten, recites our prayer: "Dear goddess, thank you for silver gray skies spanning the crumbs of Americana... for sips of pear liquor...for falling into the lap of half-hearted bliss with reflective regret, and si-mul-taneously sending me on a kayak ride into the Grand Canyon of emotion."

She says, "Goddess, teach us to love in spite of pain, to open up rather than shut down, to cultivate hope instead of bitterness, to make madmen into emperors, miracles out of beggars and maestros of the deaf."

She says, "Help us pay attention to how our feet feel every time we take a step, and to notice every sensation in our body all at once. Dear goddess, thank you for deep fried cheddar chunks covered in shredded potatoes. Thank you for the power to change my mind, even if my mind cannot change reality."

She says, "Help me take responsibility for my inner space, and to give myself permission to feel negative feelings instead of pushing them away. Let your thundering moods entice us to pray without knowing what to say or even looking for the way to say it. To be aware of our breath. To laugh without getting the joke. Dear goddess, please manifest yourself for us tonight so we can slap you on your goddamn golden goddess ass."

Amelia pauses, makes sure she didn't miss anything,

and turns to me. "How was that?"

"You forgot the stars," I say.

Amelia's laughter, when she realizes she's done something ridiculous, always stops her in her tracks. Her jaw drops and her breath falls out like tiny atom bombs.

She tucks into me to hide her gorgeous blush from the night, and rapid-fires a P.S. over my shoulder: "Dear goddess please stars now, k?"

6.

Amelia and I reach Higgins Street hours after bar time. Downtown is empty. Everyone long stumbled home.

The Greyhound Station is on Broadway. Broadway runs into Higgins, which turns into Brooks. Together these streets map out a tour of some of the most asinine roadway decisions in the country's history.

Missoula's layout is pretty simple—Higgins is the spine that holds downtown in place, and all those saloon side streets are her ribs. Her bridge leaps like a pelvis over the river, and from this juicy part of town two legs spread southward. One sticks straight out, draped in a long nylon of businesses, restaurants, banks and malls. The other leg kind of bends at the knee, propping up the University district before drooping down into a big fat K-Mart/Wal-Mart foot.

Around 15,000 years ago, the valley of Missoula belonged to some 3,000 square miles of glacial lake. Through the murky tides of change, the water left Missoula and never came back. There aren't many who can say the same.

Now only the rivers remain. The Blackfoot flows into the Clark Fork, which drives straight through the city westward out of Hellgate canyon, a cleavage in Missoula's branded hills, and on to the Bitterroot. This deadly passage brings ice floes in winter and ugly winds in any season. But the moniker "Hellgate" has nothing to do with the weather. It came from the ease with which certain natives used the canyon to ambush other natives back in the day.

One of Montana's many statutes leftover from olde-timey times says: *When seven or more Indians are gathered together, they shall be considered a part of a war party.* Fortunately, it's illegal to shoot at these groups. More than one Montana law is like the black-and-white photo of some racist great-grandfather you can't help feeling a little affection for, no matter how big of an asshole he was.

We knock at various apartments where we hope our friends still live, but no one answers. After a night of drinking, passing out becomes a game of musical couches. There's a house on Spruce Street where I can usually just walk in and find a corner to crash.

Tonight it's all full up. Two guys still awake by the fireplace take turns hitting a wooden pipe. "Huge party, man," one says through frozen breath. "You missed it. Pull up a floor."

One look from Amelia and I know she'd rather keep walking. We've both been on a bus for too long not to at least try finding somewhere cushy to sleep.

I call Missoula home, but I can't ever stick around very long. When I'm here I wish for oceans, when I'm by the ocean I just want a desert, the desert makes me miss the city, but I see tall buildings and I want my mountains back. So I wander. Deep down, I wonder where my nomadic tendencies come from. Maybe I need too much, like I want to be everywhere at once. Or I'm still looking for the perfect spot. The ideal napping place. A patch of ground that precisely fits my ass. But I can't seem to settle in anywhere. My feet move and all I can do is hang on.

Amelia and I are halfway across the bridge, right in the cusp of the canyon's prickling breeze, and she asks me, "Are you going to tell me about Vegas?"

"I might."

"You should."

"Maybe I will."

"Do it."

"It wasn't diamonds and roses."

"Stop being evasive," she says. "You're always evasive about your personal life, but this time I have you trapped on a bridge and I can throw you off. So speak. Out with it."

The truth is, I moved to Vegas to return some continuity to my life. Before Vegas I'd been living out of a truck, owned next to nothing, and slept in a different county every couple weeks.

"Well, I went down to see this possibly maybe girlfriend—" is what I tell Amelia, which is also true.

"Yes. This unnamed woman you never talk about."

"—and, uh, it didn't work out."

Love and travel both magically slow down time by zooming in and dissecting each moment, fracturing them into smaller and smaller units. Seconds seem like hours. Hours like days.

"Okay," she says. "So why didn't it work out? What did you do? Obviously you didn't come straight home."

"Um…"

"Yes?"

"Turns out she was a man?"

"I will drown you." Amelia scowls and points suggestively over the guardrail.

For some reason, Vegas became the place I hoped to rediscover continuity, to escape the cracks in the road and hide away in an endless repetition of identical days. Falling in love was a side effect.

"My heart was broken, okay? What more do you want me to say?"

Amelia clutches my elbow, letting me off the hook. "I'm sorry," she says.

I thought settling down in a strange city would fill in

the fractures; I assumed love would smooth over the cracks. But cracks appear everywhere. Now there's one in my chest, and I've followed it back home. Back to the filling station. Back to Missoula. The place where my journeys begin and end. The sanctuary where I always return and the port from which I always embark. Over and over like the salty cove tide.

"The worst part is she makes me exactly as happy as she makes me miserable," I say.

"You're hopeless," she says.

"Then things got bad."

"How so?"

"I asked her to marry me."

7.

Katie Ludwick once told me that getting a woman is the easiest thing in the world. "Just grab her and kiss her," she said.

Sounds good on paper. But the time and space between the grab and the kiss is a vast wilderness, easy to get lost, easy to make a split second mistake. The grab is aggressive, teetering on a multitude of violations. If you can transition securely from the grab to the kiss, then violence may resolve into passion, and yes, perhaps it is just that simple from there.

But there is no end to the perils of the grab. Even if the lady understands that this grab is a prelude to the kiss, and even if she wants the kiss to happen, she may instinctively resist. Her resistance may break your resolve. Your broken resolve may turn into a shift of the eyes, a stupid, stuttering half-grab awkwardness that leaves you stumbling for the words to explain the grab away before she calls the cops.

The kiss is the only possible justification for the grab.

Nor can you kiss without the grab. It's just too sneaky. And she will never put her face in a position where it can be kissed without some sort of grabby initiator. Sudden kisses unframed by the grab are comical and ridiculous. A woman opening herself up to a sudden kiss is as likely as a man spreading his legs to an oncoming foot.

"It's easy to talk to women," Katie Ludwick likes to say. "You boys make everything too complicated. Just be like: 'Hi, how are you? I am fine. I like your face. It is pretty. Nice skirt, did you make it? What are you doing? Do you want to be my friend?'"

8.

The world's most recent pregnant virgin lives in an elaborately constructed Victorian ex-brothel. Apartment number nine.

Knock, knock!

Katie is our fifth attempt. If she doesn't answer, we'll have to crash out on the abandoned couch in the alley outside her building.

As we wait, Amelia taps her toe on the concrete.

"Just because we didn't tell anyone we were coming home does not give any of them an excuse to leave us out in the cold in the middle of the night."

I knock again, softer this time. Katie Ludwick's sleepy face emerges on the other side of the glass like a lady haunted by rats. Let's call this hypothetical lady *Rat Lady.* Katie's blondish hair electrifies a tangle so tortuous it can only be a conspiracy of her dreams. Amelia and I smile and wave. Katie scrunches up her eyes and nose and scratches her head. I fear her fingers may never escape.

With her other hand, she pushes open the old door. It nearly falls off its hinges.

"What are you doing?" she asks.

"Surprise," I say.

"Hiiiiiii." Katie Ludwick's voice is a six-year-old girl in pajamas reaching out for hugs.

She brings us inside and puts Amelia on the couch. I'm fine on the floor.

"Sorry it's so late. It's his fault."

"Whatever, dude," Katie smiles. "I'm going to go back to bed."

"Sleep."

"Sleep."

It's all we want in the whole world, all three of us. Katie's place is a galaxy of blankets, and we drink our fill.

CHAPTER TWO

JACKET

Albuquerque, NM

THE FIRST TIME I LEFT Montana for the open road I found myself in Albuquerque, New Mexico, destined to fall into the arms of an older woman.

We never said a single word to each other.

I met her downtown, headed in opposite directions through shopping mall doors. I was busy staring at a new mole on my arm and she was busy looking over her shoulder. We collided. I opened my mouth to apologize, and when she did the same, I shut my mouth to let her go first. But then she shut her mouth too. Our eyes got all tangled up in a big mess right in the doorway until she smiled and shook it off and walked past me. I followed her back inside and sat across from her in a little café and bought her dinner. We didn't speak all evening. Our precedent was set. Other than fierce moments embroiled in each other's lips, those lips stayed sealed.

We shared her little house just outside of town. She worked in a coffee shop. She had flat fingers and long brown hair, and she coughed in her bathtub through the lungs of a lingering cold.

Sex replaced conversation, filling the corners of our days. Between theaters and meals and long walks, passion punctuated the passage of time. Instead of telling me about work, she would climb on top of me as if I was Everest and she was Mallory. Instead of asking her to pass me the salt at dinner, I'd toss her over the table, and when we finished she'd wink and hand me the pepper.

In the early days of our relationship, we made love as if we were planning an expedition to another solar system. As if our entire affair on Earth was training for a future life where we'd reunite as cosmic revolutionaries destined to depose some galactic despot. We worked up the scheme with our eyes and scratched out blueprints with our teeth.

Nothing compares to planning a revolution with your body. The skin is a map. Breath designates borders. Fingertips sketch out an itinerary of nonsense.

The old folks told me: *You're wasting your time on this relationship. The two of you never even talk anymore.*

We never talked to begin with, I'd say.

Wasting your youth, they insisted. *You're wasting your youth on pipe dreams and outer space and expeditions and silent romances.*

But isn't that what youth is for—to be wasted?

My youth was like a spring storm in a monastery. It was sex fully dressed in a field of noise where the faithless come to shed lingering sanctity. But when I met my silent barista, life became a calm and steady pool of silent sleep.

One morning I woke up after three weeks with her. Three weeks without sharing a single word. I was thirsty and she walked me to the door. She seemed to know what was coming, even though I did not. I'd only meant to go out for some orange juice.

She kissed my forehead and unlocked the locks and let me out.

"Goodbye," she said.

1.

I wake up on Katie Ludwick's floor with a fierce longing for bacon. So I crawl into her room to make my complaint known. Our host murmurs from beneath kelp-colored quilts, where I can see one protruding lock of orange hair. She graciously tells me to go buy some.

Sitting on the corner of Katie's enormous bed, I notice Amelia was right. Someone is missing. "Where's Adam?" I ask.

She responds almost before I finish the question. Expecting it, I guess. "I kicked him out."

Katie Ludwick and Adam Jostler had moved in together the last time I was in Missoula. We all liked

Adam and approved of him more or less. He was a gentle soul with a golden heart, bubbling with stories and obscure little facts such as: *Almonds are in the peach family,* or *Snails have been known to sleep for up to three years.* Adam stood half a dozen inches over Katie. He had long nordic tow-colored hair and a dirty blonde beard where he couched his sincere and not infrequent smile. He seemed to know everyone in town and would spend at least a little quality time with anyone he met. He made a point to recognize something pure and noble in even the most unsavory pieces of shit. He possessed the magical power to remember people's names.

"I thought things were good," I say.

Katie sniffles from beneath the blanket. Allergies. "Things were fine until I found out I was full of baby."

"Yeah, I suppose that didn't go over too well."

"Actually, I never told him."

"He doesn't know?"

"I'm sure he knows by now."

Katie sticks out a hand and slaps around her end table for Benadryl.

"So why'd you kick him out?"

When they first started dating, Adam was homeless and jobless. Born and raised in Texas, he'd moved to Butte at fifteen. He wasted a couple restless years there, never finished high school, and then hitchhiked to Missoula. He easily made friends, which was a good thing for him because he spent most nights on someone or other's couch. In the mornings he always picked up the living room, did dishes if there were any, and hit the streets. A professional house guest, Adam never had his own place, and he never had a job until he met Katie. He just lived from corner to corner, huddling over an old guitar with searing focus, wrapped around that cedar frame like a serpent around its prey.

Then he and Katie fell in love and moved in together. She supported him all summer. They shared a bed, but never went past second base. It wasn't that Katie was religious or had a thing about waiting for marriage. She just had a thing about waiting. No one really knew what she was waiting for, least of all Adam—that's what he told me, anyway.

Whatever her reasons, he was okay with it. Which was part of why she loved him. Which may have also been part of why she wouldn't have sex with him. Adam once confided in me that their love had become so entwined in the concept of not having sex that the very idea of doing it came with a heavy terror, and he'd reached the point where he wondered if it would ever happen at all.

All of this accounted in part for Katie's toleration of his freeloading. But after five months shouldering the bills, Katie finally put the matriarchal foot down and threatened to kick him the hell out if he didn't find work. So he got a job and stuck with it, and from then on he made rent every month.

"But then he started gambling again," Katie says.

"The day I found out about the baby, Adam came home and told me he lost all the rent money at Flippers. How do you gamble away 400 dollars in one day?"

"Bad habit for a parent, I guess."

"It drives me crazy because this is my life partner. I love him. I know I'm supposed to be with him—but he's an asshole. So I just started screaming at him, hitting him. Throwing shit around the room. I told him he had no balls. That he wasn't even a man."

"Ouch."

Katie's glare pops out from under the blankets. "Well, Jesus!"

"No second chance?" I say.

"This was like chance number nine."

She tells me about how she slammed the door on his apology, grabbed her rod and went out fishing. How she stayed on the river for three hours without a single bite. How she randomly recalled Montana's vestigial law that forbids single women from going fishing alone. How she couldn't get the word "caught" out of her head. She wanted to go back to the doctor's office and beat the shit out of the nurse who'd used that term in the first place. She tells me how she drove home and with tears in her eyes ordered Adam to go. He must have expected it because he'd already packed his things. Everything Adam owned could fit into one small brown backpack, a duffle bag, and his guitar case. He bore them all like growths on his body. He used his foot to open the door.

Before he left he said, *I'm sorry Katie. And I love you. I guess that's all I can say.*

Yeah well, was all she could say.

Katie blows her nose and tells me about how all he left behind was his old black rotary wall phone, which was still sitting on the coffee table beside Katie's old orange rotary wall phone—two phones that would always belong together.

"I stared at those phones long after he was gone," she says. "Just stared at them. I remember reaching out and picking up his receiver." I imagine her brushing one finger down the hive of sound holes and then setting it back on its cradle.

Katie changes the subject to push back the tears. I pretend not to notice.

"I'm hungry," she says.

"Me too."

I tell her I'm going shopping, money or no money. When I speak the bacon word, her eyes light up.

I check in with Amelia to see if she wants to join me on my quest. One tiny hand creeps out from beneath the blanket, pointing at her purse. I guess it's up to me.

2.

The simple and potent pleasure of walking down a Missoula street late in the morning hits me by the second block. It is not a pleasure you can find in either the city or the woods, but only in some place between. Neither will you find it in a brochure, a bottle, or a book. Sunlight scatters along ruptured sidewalks, torn into strips by a translucent canopy of Ash leaves. Eccentric houses unroll shaggy lawns, sleeping fences, and the remains of last week's garage sale. No two blocks are alike. If it's continuity you seek, leave it to the sidewalks, or the birdsong, or the rare and steady beat of passing cars. Walking through Missoula is the pleasure of slipping from nowhere to somewhere—

though it may be the other way around, you never know for sure, and in such carefree ignorance you swallow the secret whole.

I am struck by how in certain brief moments, within certain square feet, Missoula can smell like wilderness. I have been away for too long. My pallet is cleared, and today, for as long as I can make it last, I'll soak up the good parts of this intoxicating town, and ignore the fact that she never fails to leave a hangover.

Eight blocks from Katie's place is a local grocery referred to my clan by the straight reading of its acronym: OSFF (pronounced oss-uh-fuff). The automatic doors slide open. My beating heart drags me straight to the bacon aisle. Yes, picture it—an aisle full of bacon. I dig through the bulging bacon bin, peeking behind the secret nativity-calendar flaps for the precise ratio of fat to meat that will justify the dollar eighty-eight I am about to spend. It's Amelia's money, bless her soul, and I will not squander this gift.

So many lovely items assail me on my journey to checkout. A six pack of local micro brew for four dollars! Candy bars in their cardboard display—five for a dollar? That's right. OSFF, I could kiss you. Still, all I'm after this morning is bacon and all I can afford is bacon, and bacon is all I get. No bag, thanks. Who can't carry a package of bacon without a bag?

The last time I shopped at OSFF was only days before I fled Missoula for the coast on the long, twisty journey that would bring me to Vegas. I'd come in for a sandwich, and I ended up wandering around the aisles for two hours, carrying that sandwich the whole time. At first I thought I wanted something else, something to accompany the sandwich. Nothing looked good. Occasionally a thing would start to look good until I reached toward it or touched the packaging, but then I would recoil and move to a new aisle. Two hours of this.

That's when I knew I had to leave. In leaving Missoula, I learned to want Missoula back again, and all other mute desires rekindled within me.

3.

Back to Katie's building, I trickle down the steps and open the door. A blast of bacon scented female slaps me up the nose, along with familiar sizzles. There stands Katie Ludwick in the kitchen, gristly fork in hand, meditating upon her sacred searing strips.

"You had bacon the whole time," I gawk.

"Dude, I always have bacon."

"Why didn't you say so?"

"I forgot."

"You forgot you always have it?"

I throw the new package in the fridge with the remains of the frying package, the reserve package, and the package that's been sitting unopened for weeks.

Katie looks so beautiful standing there in smeared pajama bottoms and bulging tank top. A slim strip of belly button flesh peeks out above her waistband.

When Katie Ludwick was seventeen, she dreamed of starting a revolution. She told me she'd never get married or have kids. She said: "Single women without babies are the most powerful creatures on the planet. Men of all ages find them attractive; every woman secretly wants to be them. Every ounce of passion and love that would otherwise go to a child can go to changing the world. Mothers are narrow, single-minded creatures. When you have a baby, that's all you care about. The world doesn't matter anymore except in relation to your own stupid kid. Everyone else can go to hell as long as your baby is okay." She said, "I want to create more independence, not more need. I want to change the world, dammit."

Like most people, Katie Ludwick is made up of two contradictory selves. On one hand there's the slovenly Katie. This Katie sleeps past noon and then continues to lie in bed watching video-recorded soap operas after she wakes up. This Katie spends her days wandering through town, fishing the rivers, going to coffee shops and visiting friends.

Then there's Katie the rabid artist. When the mood strikes her, this Katie will hole up in her studio for days, painting, drawing, cutting and taping. Her art isn't anything your run-of-the-mill critic would call great, but it possesses a kind of wild imagination and raw honesty that cannot be systematically crafted. She makes collages like she's cutting out pieces of her soul. Her paintings are mad stews of dark blended colors and shuddering images, often textured with trinkets and bits of glass. She constructs Frankenstein grotesques out of random plastic toys and creepy old dolls.

One time we took an old typewriter out to the woods and blew it all to hell with a shotgun. Katie brought the pieces back home and made a sculpture. She said, "Sometimes you have to tear a thing apart so its soul can get out."

Katie also draws cartoon stick figures. These are my favorite. They look like little kid drawings, but somehow this huge depth of expression and meaning flies out from between the skinny lines. And they're hilarious. My favorite is a quick pencil drawing of two deformed little monsters. A copy of this sketch still lives on a piece of orange paper in a tiny corner of my backpack. One creature says, "Hello, alien," and the other replies, "Hello, freak." She once did a sketch of three monsters, the littlest of whom tells the others to "Quit looking drunk."

When I consider Katie's virgin pregnancy, I always think of her art. How her lazy-self teams up with her artistic-self, and her best work seems to come from her slightest efforts. She wills things into existence with natural ease, almost as an afterthought, like pulling a rabbit out of a hat. Maybe her fetus came from the same place.

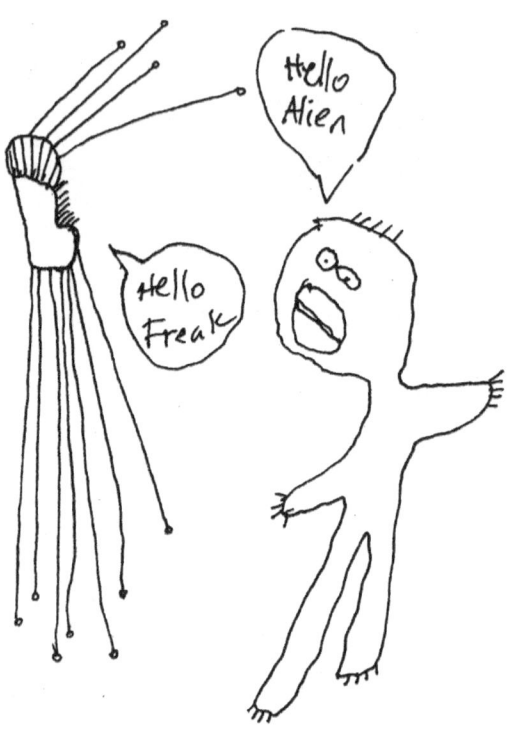

4.

"Or maybe you were abducted—you know, by aliens. Maybe you're a host."

Katie Ludwick wrinkles up her forehead and frowns, as she does with most of my suggestions.

"So I'm going to have an alien baby?" she says.

"Well, it wouldn't necessarily be a bad thing—I mean, these aliens would have to be pretty smart to pull it off. It'd be a superhuman child, genetically advanced. Maybe he'll lead humanity into the stars."

"She."

"What?"

"She's a girl."

"You got an ultrasound?"

Katie stabs a strip of bacon. "No. I just know."

The way she looks at me now reminds me of a tired old sea turtle, 200 years old and ready for its next incarnation.

"I read about this old sea turtle who raised a group of orphan hippos," I say.

"No shit?"

"No shit."

I pull a shrieking teakettle off the stove and hunt around for cups.

"I want to go to a foreign country," Katie says. "And when I get there I'll go around saying blah blah blah to people on the street and nobody will know the difference."

This feels like the perfect moment to ask, "Where's my jacket?"

"What jacket?"

"My torn up blue jacket—the boxing jacket. The infamous jacket of utter coziness. What do you mean, *what jacket*?"

"That's my jacket," she says.

"I'm reclaiming it. Where is it?"

She holds the fork up to my face, glistening pig flesh scrolling at the corners. "I lent it to my brother. Here, eat this."

"I haven't seen him wear that jacket since high school." I bite the bacon. It is, in fact, delicious.

"Oh yeah. It was his jacket first. I almost forgot."

"It's my jacket," I say. "He gave it to me."

"He gave it to me before he gave it to you," Katie counters. "Here, eat this."

Meanwhile, Amelia is in the living room trying on all of Katie's clothes.

"What are you doing?" I ask.

"I'm trying on all of Katie's clothes. Someone talked me into ditching my bag last night."

"That looks good," I say.

Amelia drowns a yellow Dixie's Diner shirt beneath a hulking black hoodie. "It looks good on Katie. Not on me."

As Amelia strips back down to her underwear she shouts, "How can you be pregnant if you're a virgin?"

"Word on the street is you have to be one or the other," I add.

Katie's voice crawls back from the kitchen. "You guys are geniuses."

Amelia climbs into a pair of stained Carhartts and says, "Well, are you pregnant or aren't you?"

"Obviously."

"And you're really a virgin."

"Yes."

"You and Adam seriously never had sex?"

Katie's head pokes around the corner. She wields her fork like a trident. "I wasn't ready," she says.

"Are you sure he didn't—you know… like, when you were drunk or passed out or something?"

"No," Katie gives us one of her patented death glares. "Adam would never do that. Anyway, the doctor checked me out. I'm intact."

"Did the doctor have a theory?"

Katie's situation reminds me of the French film, *Léolo*. Léolo believed that his own conception resulted from his mother falling into a cart of inseminated tomatoes.

"I could tell she didn't want to think about it. She acted like it was no big deal."

"I'm sure she's confident the facts will eventually yield to common sense," I say.

Back down to nothing but matching purple bra and panties, Amelia rushes to the bathroom. As she passes by Katie, she opens her mouth and Katie delivers the bacon. Bathroom door slams.

Katie tends to her sizzling stove, and I'm left in the living room staring out the windows. After a minute, I hear the click of a burner shutting off. Katie shuffles up beside me, carrying a scuffed-up water bottle and a yellow apple.

"Now I know why people have sex," she says.

"Oh yeah?"

"So when they get knocked up, even if they've been slutting around with the entire congregation, at least they can say the father is one of these guys. Maybe they don't know who and maybe they really don't care, but at least he's someone. But I don't get to do that. Instead, I have to say there is no father, and put up with the kind of cross examination you guys are giving me now."

She tells me she later considered having sex with Adam just to avoid confusion, but she'd already kicked him out of the house. She'd told him not to call her, to just leave her alone. Wouldn't've been any big deal if she wasn't still in love with him.

"I wonder what he thinks," I say.

"Probably that I cheated on him. Which is fine, because maybe that makes him feel better about the breakup." Katie cradles her water bottle to her breast. Practicing, I reckon.

The bathroom door flies open. Amelia emerges in a loose bathrobe, a pair of Pokemon PJs, and a v-neck t-shirt. "This will have to do," she says.

"There's something called parthenogenesis," I tell Katie. "I looked it up. It's a form of reproduction without fertilization. It occurs naturally sometimes with aphids, bees, scorpions, fish. Even a few birds, I think."

"I'm not a fish," Katie Ludwick says.

"Yeah, I know."

The challenge of finding ways to make sense of her situation surpasses my abilities.

I say, "Just think about all the virgin births in mythology. Some beautiful examples. Take Lao Tzu for instance. Conceived when his mother saw a falling star. That's a nice story."

"Can we not talk about this anymore?" Katie says.

Amelia leans over last night's makeshift bed and gathers up all the shrapnel from around where she dropped her purse. "Do you have a coat? I need a coat. I'm a coat person."

"What about the coat you were wearing last night?"

"Does it look like last night to you?"

"I'll go get your bag," I say.

"No, I've got a ride coming. Here, give me hugs. I'm going outside." Amelia bounces over a pile of jeans and wraps her arms around my neck. Her perfume smells almost funny amidst the fat frying ambiance. She squeezes me stork-like, one foot dangling in the air.

Out she goes, cigarettes in hand, to wait in the alley. Out of my life as quick as she came in. Always that woman is walking away, following whatever dot her eyes have affixed upon the horizon, always leaving me with words on my lips. For the life of me, I don't know what those words are.

5.

At Katie's request, I put on some music. Donovan is morning music. Breakfast-making music. *Colors, Catch the Wind, Season of the Witch*. When the bacon is ready we segue into the Ramones. We sit side-by-side on the couch and crunch leathery pig flesh to the hiss of a dying cassette tape.

"Welcome home," Katie says.

"Thanks," I say. "How've you been?"

"Fat."

"You look good."

"I'm glowing, apparently."

"Where's your brother?"

Katie laughs. "You really want that jacket."

"Yes."

"I don't know. He's probably at Flippers."

When I leave, Amelia is still outside waiting. I catch her by the elbow on the stairs. Her toes tap the concrete and I touch her arm. She stops and turns and does not speak. Her mind is full of complicated games I can only crash through in strange sidewalk moments. She takes one step back toward me. Without really knowing why, I lean in to deliver a kiss. She follows my lead for a split second, but then her head darts away, gazing down like a street lamp at my blemished brown boots.

"Hmm," she says.

"What?"

"Just, hmm."

She pulls out a cigarette and lights it with a pink lighter. I notice speckled fingernail polish for the first time. "I am a broken machine," she says. "Let's go to the river."

"Now?"

"Yes…No… YES!"

I glance down the alley at the Flippers Casino sign. My jacket is only yards away, I'm sure of it!

"No," she says. "My ride will be here any minute."

I feign a dramatic tone. "We'd never make it, anyway."

"It's only two blocks away," she pouts. "I can smell it. Let's go. We'll play break the river."

"What's that?"

"You stand in the river with a rock or a tree branch or whatever, and you smash it. You try to break off pieces of the river. First person to break the river in half wins."

"This is an actual game?"

"Sometimes it's important to do something futile," she says.

"Find me later tonight. We'll go."

Amelia glances up, her eyes popping with fireworks. "I will find you," she says, "and you can tell me all about your torrid affair with the Vegas Girl."

Las Vegas, NV

I first met her under the gasp of a clear winter night. I was still unfamiliar with the city, so I was half trying to find my way back to my apartment and half trying to identify the few stars peeking through the eerie magenta Vegas haze. She was kneeling down in the street and I didn't see her at all. I nearly tripped over her legs. Then I tried to step around her like she was road construction.

"Hey, listen to this," she said. Her head was sideways on the ground, earlobe caressing a manhole cover. "Down here."

I glanced around, clearing my throat.

"Water," she said.

I stood there without words. I could tell she was sexy, even in the dark.

"You can't hear it from up there. Come down on the ground."

I crouched down beside her and tilted my head. I heard it. Gushing running dirty sewer water. I'd never listened to the sounds beneath the streets before, never bothered to try. She stared at me with the jewel of her eyes as we knelt crook-headed on the iron platter, our noses inches apart. She beamed at the sound. Her eyes darted back and forth like an optical lens across a CD. I smiled at her. Couldn't have stopped if I'd wanted to. "People live down there," she whispered.

"What people?" I whispered back, conforming to whisper's infection.

"Homeless people. The mayor says we don't have any, but that's because he hides them away. They all live underground."

"Oh."

We knelt there for a long time, listening, staring, silently planning out our next few months together, months that became a mythology of opposites in the spaces between words. By the following week we were inseparable. Even the nights we spent apart were bound by phone calls, letters, schemes to impress and surprise the other, agreements to both stare up at the moon at such-and-such a time.

I once delivered a box full of bouncy balls to her door

with instructions to tip them all at once down a hill.

She disguised herself with a short blonde wig and glasses, set me on a chase through the city, clue after clue, until I found her in a bakery, hiding behind a newspaper like some sort of Russian spy in an old movie.

We traded dreams. I wrote her stories. She drew me pictures. I gave her baths and cooked her dinner. She found it all delicious and climbed over piles of dishes to cling to my ribs. She's the only woman I thought maybe I could have babies with.

I'd have bet every casino on the Strip it would never end.

6.

Flippers Casino isn't even a block away from Katie's house. Just kitty-corner across the alley. Somehow I still end up seeing someone I know before I reach the parking lot. It has begun. They will pop up everywhere now. Who can say how many I'll meet at Flippers! In a town of people who know people, this bar is a veritable den of everybody who knows everybody.

This one is William. We've been friends since high school. He's on his way to pick up today's ration of coffee and cigarettes. When he spots me his eyes widen behind his glasses, and as he comes to a theatrical stop both of his arms spring up to point me into existence.

"You're back!"

"Yes."

"So, um..."

"Flippers."

"Okay, I'll be right there, just have to get coffee," and he dashes off.

Describing Flippers is as hard as describing my mom. She's too familiar to begin breaking her into pieces, and it's almost uncomfortable to try. All I can say is that Flippers is nothing if not dim. Thin strips of neon weave a highway between flashing beer signs. Most of the rare illumination is provided by the jukebox next to the door, with a little extra from whatever blinky lights escape from the keno machines.

I grab the handle, do not turn it, and tug. Years ago someone broke the latch and it stayed that way for so long that when Flippers' management got around to fixing it, none of the regulars could figure out what to do. Every single one of us who attempted entry after the fix, resorting to our habitual pulling or pushing, would freeze for a moment of total panic, wondering if either a) Flippers had shut down, or b) we were trapped forever, depending on which side of the door we stood. No one learned any better. Drunkenness thrives on habit. Instinct shoves its way past coordination and rational thought, insisting that if it can't find the way, no one can. And no one ever thought to *use* the handle. We'd just bang on the door until a bartender let us in. Finally, management decided they'd better break the latch again, and they did, and thank God for that.

And so, with a yank but not a twist, I enter a land of keno machines, cheap wine, and tall tables.

Dennis works behind the bar, grinning at me from the other side of his Groucho mustache. I don't think I've ever seen that man's lips. Dennis' mustache is a pair of eight-inch forearms folded across a barrel chest. Without it I'd put Dennis at about five-foot-six. With it, he's six-foot-nine.

"Hi Josh!"

He buys me a beer just for being gone so long and asks me about my trip. Some small talk ensues.

"Is Ludwick here?" I ask.

"Yeah, he's over there somewhere losin' money," Dennis says.

I glance over among the keno machines. I can hear the sound of numbers flashing; I can see the old ladies melting into their chairs, fixated upon glowing screens like those podlings from the Dark Crystal parting with their essence.

"Did he have a jacket on?" The question is for drama's sake, and to heighten my anticipation. "It's sort of a light blue denim boxer's jacket."

"What's a boxer's jacket?"

"Is he wearing any jacket at all?"

Dennis has no idea. He laughs at me and says, maybe.

7.

I CREEP AMONG THE MACHINES and their regulars. Flippers houses some dusty old gems. The type who take pride in their backwoods alcohol-fueled inheritance and remain humble about the literacy and insight they've acquired in spite of it.

Missoulians are an odd breed. Out here you can throw a rock in a crowd and good chance you'll hit one of the metal-loving neo-hippie deer-hunting earth-firster redneck liberal vegans who grow their own bok choy, drive trucks, and serve up modern dance with their football. The kind who own multiple firearms and still vote for gun control; who personally find homosexuality gross, but will fight to the bones to defend gay marriage; who don't believe in global warming, but recognize that alternative energy is still a smart idea; who think we sure as hell should have bombed someone after 9/11, but why Iraq for Chrissakes?!

Smoke rises from an ashtray near an empty wine glass at the far end of the room. Dean has keno-vision and does not notice my approach. He wears a black t-shirt, no jacket. I flank him until I can see the glowing machine image miniaturized onto his glasses.

After watching him lose a few credits, I say, "The secret is to bet up just before you win."

"I'm trying," Dean replies without looking at me. He raises his bet and clicks. Numbers flash. Three out of seven. Not good enough.

"Don't you have these things figured out yet?"

"I figured out they take in more than they pay out," he says.

"And yet you keep playing."

"I'm a machine that pays out more than it takes in."

"Sounds like a match made in heaven," I say.

"Hey did I tell you what happened to me the other day?"

This is how things are with me and Dean. I've been away for months, but instead of saying, *Wow! Welcome home. How was your trip?* he dives into a story about his day. C.S. Lewis said the mark of genuine friendship is when two people, separated for any number of months or years, can reunite as if no time has passed at all. The conversation picks up right where it left off.

He's shaved his head since I last saw him. Prickles of hair just starting to grow back. His shrubby red beard hangs off freckled cheeks and nestles around his thin lips like an old grandpa cradling a remote control.

Dean wiggles his fingers at the screen. He places his bet.

"Zo-zee-zaz!" he says.

"What's that, some sort of magic spell?"

"Christian magic," he says, and repeats *Zozezaz* with even more flamboyance. "It's a Gnostic invocation to elude alien overlords who try to block the soul's ascent to the transcendent God."

"And it works on keno?"

"These damned machines impede my journey! I say Zozezaz, brother! Look at that. Twenty credits. You have to use the right numbers, though. See how 11, 19, 33, and 49 were all hits?"

"Obviously."

"You should check out the Coptic diagrams," Dean says. "They're like ancient electrical schematics."

"You were going to tell me about your day?"

"Oh, right." Dean picks new numbers. "So I was walking across the bridge. I saw an osprey swoop down to grab a fish out of the river. Just then I passed a bum. He asked me for change. I gave him everything I had—something like two bucks—and I said, *Did you see the osprey?* Guess what he said."

"I have no idea"

"He said, *I baptize you in the name of the fish*, and

then he threw all my money over the railing. We both leaned over and watched it hit the water."

This kind of thing happens to Dean all the time. Sometimes I wonder how much is his imagination. Sometimes Dean wonders the same thing.

"Weird," I say. "Then what?"

"Then we went our separate ways."

"And you came to Flippers and won fifty bucks?"

"No," he says. "I didn't have any money left. I just went home."

"That's kind of anti-climactic."

"Wrong. Backwards. The whole story is one free-falling climax!"

I take our glasses up to the bar for refills, free to gamblers. When I return, Dean's up over two hundred nickels.

8.

DEAN LIVES IN A NEBULOUS zone between mastery over his surroundings and absolute dissociation with reality. He married this woman once, a few years back. They'd dated for over a year, then they got married and divorced three months later. They moved to Portland, which is where everything fell to shit. Dean said she changed on a dime, like someone flipped a switch, or the wedding ring severed a crucial psychic tripwire. Their relationship disintegrated within weeks, but he kept living in the apartment with her and her new boyfriend until he could afford to go back home. When the boyfriend moved in, Dean moved to the couch. They jammed together sometimes. "He was pretty cool," Dean said.

By the time he got back to Missoula, Dean was seeing prophecies and conspiracies everywhere. There's no doubt he'd gone over the emotional edge. Delusions and false memories infiltrated his daily life. Something like an overdrive of the imagination, or a subconscious attempt to construct an alternate reality to the one he'd lived through. Maybe the rational side of his brain—which has always dug his best trenches—was overcompensating.

Pieces of his stories were probably true, and pieces of them probably weren't. For a while he thought he was under FBI surveillance. Later he got it into his head he was the "Red Brother" of Hopi prophecy—and it was his job to go to the southwest and save the world. He took a bus to Arizona, stayed with the Hopi until they told him to go away. Nothing dramatic happened. No gathering of the masses, no flashes of insight, no car chases. He just went, told them he was on a mission, and came home.

But I've never been able to shake the feeling that maybe he did save the world. You can't really prove he didn't, and well, we're all still here.

9.

"Where's my jacket?" I ask.

"What jacket," Dean says.

"The old comfy blue one. Katie told me she gave it to you."

"Uh... I think it's at home."

"Cash out and buy us some fries."

Dean wavers. He doesn't like to walk away until he's either doubled his money or lost it all.

Up comes Will, returning with coffee to rescue Dean from his moral dilemma. Will's a handsome chap with short dark hair and the most heightened sense of wonder I've ever known. Kids in high school labeled him a computer geek because they didn't know any better. But he isn't nearly as excited about computers themselves as the things you can do with them.

"I have returned! You're gambling?"

"He's gambling. I'm starving."

"Don't go anywhere. I'm getting a drink."

Dean keeps up the keno, kicking into high gear. He's betting the maximum. We watch his credits tumble toward zero. Then he hits five out of seven and the rapid clicks of victory run it all back up to equilibrium.

"So you saw my sister," Dean says.

"Yeah, I crashed there last night."

"How's she doing?"

"Looks about ready to pop," I say.

"That's what she gets for staying a virgin so long."

"Your dad should have warned her."

Dean yawns into a stretch, looks like he's about to cash out, thinks better of it, and bets big.

"Pregnancy suits her," I say. "She looks good."

"Pregnant? Who's pregnant?"

Will bounces back with a cold mug of Roscoe's. Froth sparkles on his lips, thickening his perpetual five o'clock shadow.

"Katie."

Will suspends the moment by sneezing into the breast of his jacket. A single sniffle follows, and he says, "Katie's pregnant?"

"Yep."

"Why didn't I know this? Since when?"

"About eight months," says Dean.

"I'm so out of the loop," says Will.

"Dean thinks it's the second coming."

"Maybe," Dean corrected. "Odds are the second coming was already aborted."

"I thought Jesus was supposed to return full grown and ready for a fight."

"What if the Antichrist was aborted?"

"That would put a wrinkle in the pro-life movement."

"I can see the headlines: *Abortion saves the Universe.*"

Dean says, "Okay, I'm done." He's run all his credits down to nothing. Well, almost nothing. Cashes out with a single credit and places the ticket in front of the buzzing blue screen.

"For luck," he says.

10.

We emerge squinting from the Flippers dungeon into the light of noon and settle into three plastic patio chairs. The conversation continues apocalyptically onward. I feel a welling joy at the bliss which comes from trying to puzzle out the inscrutable. I've been gone too long from other minds, trapped too deeply within the succubus of pacing and useless thoughts.

Dean begins: "If the world is a sequence of orderly events, like an interconnected Rube Goldberg machine tumbling forth from a precise, premeditated configuration, then the ending must be inherent in the beginning. Encoded, if you will—"

"I will," I say.

"No," William puns, "*I* Will."

"—Like the way DNA unfolds into a living organism."

Will jumps in with more detail. "You mean like how a gene interacts with its environment to produce observable phenotypes—" He interrupts himself with one lonely, violent hiccup. Will is the only man I've ever met whose hiccups are isolated rather than chronic: here a random antisocial hiccup dripping with paranoia, there a sociopath sniper hiccup in a bell tower. He continues, "—and these are epiphenomenon you'll never actually find one-to-one correspondences to in the DNA."

How did so many concepts wind up in one brain? Will just reads. And reads.

Across the parking lot stands the greatest low-budget apartment complex in town, a flop palace for starving artists and fizzling musicians. I crashed there for a few months the first time I dropped out of college, sleeping on a tiny orange air mattress in the corner of a friend's room. Glancing at all the little trinkets and candles perched on the rows of windowsills, the strings of beads and slung tie-dyed tapestries, I am struck by how familiar it all seems. All those default decorations of life straight out of high school, when you're just learning how to take care of yourself, before you have the first clue what you really want.

"Exactly," Dean stabs a finger into the air. "And since our entire lives are reducible to a long sequence of only four unique molecules, mightn't the end of civilization be just so encoded in the ancient kabalas and prophecies of madmen?"

Lately I've been feeling like I'm stuck right on the edge of what I want. Like up to this very moment I've been living a knock-off version of my dreams.

"It could happen," Dean continues, "Self-fulfilling prophecy. Fanatics and politicians. Too much power in the hands of someone who thinks they're the voice of god. Someone who reads every current event into some old text."

Will leans down to slide a striped yellow dress sock up his shin. "They believe in Armageddon, and so they try to make it happen."

Lately I feel less like an entity and more like a pile of parts, a sequence of gears. Dean, despite delusional segues, has always been just the opposite, fundamentally unchangeable. I sometimes think Dean will spend the rest of his life in Missoula, hunched over a desk conducting intricate patterns in ink, tracing my orbits with his art as I bounce around the world.

"Are we saying the world can't end on its own?"

Will diverts the subject: "Could it have *begun* on its own?"

I love to watch them fence this way.

Dean gets that tone in his voice like he'd intended this turn in the conversation all along. "Of course. The world couldn't help but begin."

Lately I've come to realize that everything I want to know about, I know in fragments. Because my life is a jigsaw puzzle. But one where even if everything gets set down in the right order, none of the pieces touch. An illusion of happiness, vapid reflections on the surface of a pond, haggard from ripples and wrinkles. Old age is just an afternoon nap away. Then where will I be? Happy from all the chasing? Sitting on the porch with a handful of disjointed dreams.

"What do you mean?" Will asks. His mouth is agape, anticipating a sneeze that refuses to erupt.

"Isn't it obvious? Okay, answer this: what was here before the universe?"

"God?" says Will.

"Another universe?" I try.

Dean's eyebrows buckle. Will has caught him off-guard. He turns in his chair. "God? I thought you were an atheist."

Will stares longingly into his empty pint glass, watching the foam slake down the sides. "So what if I am? Maybe I'm an atheist who believes in God."

Thinking back, I'm pretty sure this edge I'm on has been right there in front of me the whole time. Like the world's horizon, or a mirage that moves forward when you move forward, and stops when you stop. Happiness is the carrot dangling from a stick fused to your spine, and chasing it is as productive as trying to jump out of your own shadow.

Dean laughs, "Out West there's not much difference between those who believe in God and those who don't."

Unless chasing happiness *is* happiness…

"Jesus was an atheist, you know."

"You should make it your life's mission to prove that."

"Maybe I will."

Sandwiched between the mystic and the scientist, I adopt the role of keeping things on track. "Okay let's get back to this theory that the world couldn't help but begin."

"It's simple!" Dean leaps to his feet and begins to pace. "Trace backward to the void. Nothingness— right? Well, it's no great leap to get from nothing to something."

"How so?"

Maybe true happiness is a well-aged disappointment you get to drink when you're old.

"Easy. If there's nothing existing, then there's nothing to stop things from popping into existence. No laws of physics, no barriers, no forces, no fences. Not even logic."

Will thinks it over. "So, if nothing; therefore something—is that what you're saying?"

Maybe true happiness comes not from getting what you want; but from wanting what you don't really want, and then not getting it.

Dean rakes four fingers through the red tentacles of his beard. "Of course, once things start existing, then you quickly build up a system of limitations. The rules congeal. You get things that won't let any other things take up the same space. You get laws of motion and interaction. By the time you reach recorded history it's hard to come up with anything new."

Will ponders this and slurps down the final few gathering drops of beer.

Whatever my younger self wanted, or thought he wanted living in the squalor of that apartment across the alley, I've long forgotten. But whatever it was, I don't think I got it—and I'm just going to go ahead and thank my lucky stars for that.

"There's supposed to be a party tonight somewhere," Dean says.

"Where?"

"Not sure. I just heard a rumor."

"Music?"

"Probably."

"Ladies?"

"Of course!"

"Sounds wild."

I want to go. I want to chase what I don't want—

"It's something to do…"

—and not get it.

11.

WE CIRCLE A FEW MORE blocks, tell some jokes, and pose a few riddles. I walk back to Katie's house after an embarrassing four straight losses to Will's superior riddle medicine. Dean goes the other way, on a quest for medicine of his own. He promises to bring my jacket by later.

Katie's door is unlocked, but the place is empty. She's left a note: *Gone to the doctor. Do whatever you want. Love, Katie.*

Whatever I want, huh? Katie's den of slovenly delight clutches at me like a child digging through a pile of puppies. The sink is full of grimy, sleeping dishes. The floor is an archipelago of dirty clothes, quilts, and art supplies.

I spot a spatula poking out between couch cushions. I liberate it with one swift tug, recalling Excalibur, and notice it is clean. How a clean spatula got from the kitchen to the couch I refuse to guess. I hold it to the light. One corner has melted flat from careless usage, a grotesque plastic tumor, a hunchback, a spot of leprosy. I feel its self-conscious gaze.

Oh spatula, you are devastated and deformed, but still as useful as ever. Shall I aspire to impart unto you the secrets of space and time?

I explain to the spatula that of all the things Katie and I share, our deepest connection is this: we both make a point of trusting something invisible and spontaneous to take care of us. I can't count how many times money has arrived out of the blue precisely as needed, or how often food seemed to barrel down the street in search of some hunger to fill. My parents once lived this way, too. At some point you stop—I guess when the novelty wears off, or when you decide it's just luck and your number's about to come up.

"But until then, spatula," I say, "there's magic ripe for the grabbin'. It's in the air and it's attracted to motion."

Somehow this cosmic medicine prefers a moving target. Stick your head out of a car window and feel the breeze.

"It's a Jesus lifestyle, spatula. *The son of man has no place to lay his head.* He was a nomad who thought people should live in the moment. I've met more Atheists on the road living like the man and not even realizing it; and more Christians who've devoted their lives to securing a luxurious place to lay their heads."

They live by balance-books, nine-to-fives, and holiday vacations, trapped in schedules and budgets while they sport their WWJD bracelets. But Jesus said not to worry about tomorrow. Tomorrow will take care of itself.

"Don't bury your head in the future, spatula!" I shout, "Don't fret about heaven and eternal salvation—for eternity is here and salvation is now, not in some abstract tomorrow waiting a ways off down the line. Faith does not save you; faith *is* salvation. Love does not get us into heaven; love *is* heaven. To love and hope and believe is to enter immediately through the gates. Don't confuse the passport for the country, spatula. Don't mistake the map for the territory. Heaven runs parallel to all premeditated paths. Go one step out of your way to help a stranger and you're there. You've transcended time and space and self. What sort of nebulous eternal realm can compete with that?"

The spatula does not reply. I assume it's carefully considering the question. I walk to Katie's desk and push the flat of the spatula against a disheveled stack of papers. I scramble them up a bit. The stack seems in no better or worse order than before.

"Okay, spatula, forget the spiritual side. Just look at it from a practical point of view. An empty wallet is not that bad. Hell, being broke is actually pretty good these days. Most Americans are in debt, and compared to a big fat debt, zero is a pretty big number."

People end up in debt out of fear they will one day have nothing.

But having nothing is so damned cheap.

Granted, it still costs more to be poor, but it's worse if you're sedentary, trying to raise a family and keep the basics maintained. It's why you find the one-day-at-a-time lifestyle in so many unexpected places: folks out on the road, hitchhiking, biking, walking, jostling along in old beat-up cars with great mileage. They realize the world is full of stuff, and you can go out and open your mouth wide, and as long as you keep walking, the rain will fall in. It's like Dean's theory of creation. The more you have, the less you're open to receive. Possessions ultimately dispossess. Bound and saddled you can no longer move fluidly through a fluid world.

Spatula and I circle the room, blessing objects with a light touch from his gnarled melty corner. We bless a baby doll. Katie has blackened in her eyes, dreaded out her hair, and stapled trinkets to her arms. The front end of a Tonka truck explodes from her stomach. We bless a stuffed moose and a rotting avocado. Each blessed object gets a front-row seat on the couch. I've lined them all up—dolls, toys, journals, plates, records, stamps, toothpaste, a bottle of witch hazel, a ball of string. Spatula understands now. He has seen the light, and together we propound our holy sermon.

"The people of earth were never cut out for this sedentary lifestyle," I say. "Millions of years of evolution, fine tuning these beautiful nomadic legs, and in less than two hundred years we've folded them up and put them away under our laptops. We weren't meant to sit in chairs and hide in holes. The wanderer's legacy is too strong, too rooted in the DNA, and it will roam whether we like it or not, if not physically then psychologically. And if we don't move our legs, that spirit will smoke and spin and whirl like a clutched axle. Dislodged gears burning up and burning out!"

But what can we do? There's already so many of us, and more coming down the pipelines every minute. Won't be long until we top ten billion. We're running out of room fast. Do we just pack tighter and tighter? Try to sit more still? Or is it possible to maintain momentum in some sort of coordinated way?

"We need a new method, my little friends," I proclaim. "Rugged individualism may have worked out okay on the frontier, but we humans we're fresh out of frontiers. The world washed us westward until we ran into the farther shore, and then all the rules changed. The system fed back in on itself. We didn't hit the launch in time." I keep brushing shoulders with old men running on grumpy because there's no more wilderness to steal, stockpiling guns as if any arsenal could protect them from the information infrastructure.

Times change. And what I like about Missoula is how she balances on the cusp of change without letting herself drown in it. One foot forward, ready to adapt, one foot firmly rooted where we came from. Missoula is a filter for letting through all the good parts of our steel-nosed pioneer legacy, while driving back the tides of inertia that keep what might have once been good ideas chugging along past the point of usefulness.

From the couch my congregation nods and smiles as the spirit fills their plastic nooks and ceramic bits. "I have to tell you, my brothers and sisters, I, too, feel the stale rust seeping in. The dread of motion, the dread of standing still. Sometimes I can't tell which is which and it scares me out of my mind. What if the doors fly open —and rather than me going out, something else comes in? What if I stay in one place too long and the rest of the world rushes on without me? What if in my haste it dissolves into nothingness?"

As if it all weren't already some dream.

And what the hell would I do, anyway, if I ever found a place suitable to stay put? Would I settle down? Cook breakfast? Sleep under the stars? Find a woman? Build a cabin? Grow old. Die. I could spend the rest of my life searching for the perfect view overlooking some ideal patch of grass on which to settle in and sink beneath the weeds. The rush of the wind, a gentle rain. These icons of what it means to have been alive in a world. Surrounded by the trinkets of our past, the towers of unopened boxes packed with so many memorable days never again brought to mind. Then at last, tucked-in best as can be, to etch that moment onto a gravestone and experience nothing more forever.

My arm drops to my side. The spatula slips from my grasp and finds a new home on the floor between a beanbag chair and a milk crate. I don't even remember what point I was trying to make.

I stare at Katie's disaster of an apartment; realizing the chaotic placement of all these particles came from a catalog of tiny decisions, brief moments of near-intention. Euphoria floods my brain, brought on by a frenzy of solitude, and in this single instant I think I could die content. That's the signpost of pure bliss. That's when you know it can't get any better.

But it doesn't last. The moment you reach the top of the mountain, there's only so much ogling over the panorama before it's time to climb back down. Instead of dying I turn on some music and sit among my congregation on the couch. Before long the song ignites my restless legs. I don't want to just sit around waiting for life to come to me. Should I walk to the door and open it? Nothing out there but the whole entire world. Nothing but footsteps and a million roads going everywhere. Confusion, headaches, heartaches mixed in. It's a symptom of freedom to be enslaved by endless possibility.

So I pick up a brush and dip it in oil, and I smear stupid purple lines on a piece of paper.

Life is governed by the hours, and hours are governed by the sun. The sun is governed by immeasurable spaces between the tiny vibrations of matter. I should be so small, to look outward with longing eyes, so that everything I see becomes vast potentiality. But if I am the sum of my experiences, then I am also the clouds, the mountains, the television, and every sliver under the skin turning animals into cyborgs, reconstructing world from world, smushing putty under the thumb and then stretching again to plod through the leeward side of the tip of my tongue.

Fuck it. I'm going out.

CHAPTER THREE

THE OXFORD

Prescott, AZ

YEARS AGO, I FELL for this gorgeous redhead while waiting in line at a grocery store. She stood in front of me, digging for coupons. I thought to myself, *Sweet stardust, that's one sexy lady!*

A bored checkout clerk slid her groceries over the beeping glass. He would be the liaison for my seduction, and he didn't even know it. I leaned across the conveyor belt and whispered like a tornado in a drainpipe, "Hey, do you see the woman over there? The one digging for coupons?"

My eyes darted suggestively femaleward. Yes, just like two little round darts.

"Uh," the clerk hesitated, wondering whether he

should warn me about my volume control.

"That's right," I said. "The pretty one. The one you are currently ringing up. There is no other woman anywhere near us. I suppose you'll be giving her a receipt soon."

"Yeah," he intoned. Oh, did he intone.

"Do you think I've got a chance with her?" I said. "I mean, do you think she'd ever go to dinner with me?"

"Hm…"

He'd need something cleverer than that. I was sinking here and I couldn't do this alone.

Then he said, "Well, she bought mostly frozen dinners, so she may be hard up for a decent meal."

That's more like it.

"Good point," I said. "I'll have to take her somewhere nice. But she's a knockout. Just look at her. She probably has a boyfriend, huh?"

I could hear her chuckling into her purse.

Our clerk said, "Maybe. No wedding ring, though. And I don't get the sense she's shopping for two."

He was really getting into this.

"Well, I'm going to go for it," I said. "Damn the torpedoes. Listen, I'm a little shy when it comes to talking with women. What do you say you let me write my phone number on the receipt before you hand it to her? Can you do that? Does it break any transaction laws?"

"I could lose my job," he said with all seriousness, scanning three coupons in succession.

"Maybe, but this could be the real thing. You don't want to spend the rest of your life wondering if you let something as silly as minimum wage get in the way of true love."

"You make a strong case."

Our clerk rang up the total. I still remember that magic number, $27.44.

I waited in silence, fidgeting with my can of honey-roasted peanuts and a bag of carrots. I could have gone through the express lane that day, but for some reason I did not. It wasn't even the thought: *Who needs express lanes?*, or anything like that. I'd simply stepped into the regular lane and there she was.

She paid by check. The clerk glanced at her ID.

"Thank you, Miss," he said.

Then he yawned, stretched, and with the sort of mock secrecy that is painfully obvious, tore her receipt from the register and handed it to me.

I scrawled down my name and number.

"I think there's been some mistake," I said, surreptitiously handing the receipt back to him. "This isn't mine."

"You're right," he said. "How stupid of me."

The clerk gave the receipt to the woman. She turned toward me, and, without a word, offered me her grocery bags. I donned the cap of chivalry and carried them to her car, leaving my peanuts and carrots behind. She opened the passenger door, and I set her bags on brown vinyl and white dog hair.

"You have a dog?" I asked.

"He's an Airedale," she said.

I watched her put the receipt in her purse. Then we both worked through a bunch of coy glances and awkward shiftings of weight. She parted her lips, and I got this feeling she was about to sing.

"You should call me sometime," she said.

"Okay," I said. But I didn't have her number; she had mine. As she got in her car and drove away, I decided it wouldn't have been a horrible idea to point that out.

1.

My mind roars with the destinationless thrill of motion. Leaving my spatula and plush congregation behind, I make for the bridge. When I'm close enough to hear the white roar of the river below, I get slapped by a five-year-old's need to piss. I can hear my mother's voice in my head telling me I should've gone before I left the house. I don't really want to backtrack all the way to Katie's, and there's an alley behind Flippers that'll do the trick.

I hobble back across the street, knees clenched, doing the peepee-jog. It occurs to me that a man repressing his nature always looks a little like a jackass.

For the last few steps I give up all pretense and dash into the alley, where a flimsy blue dumpster slumps like a dead whale on the sand.

I shift back and forth. My thighs jiggle. If my zipper were a bra-clasp, I would not have fumbled more. Finally free, I prop myself against the lid, cock in hand, counting off the distance from my bladder to the ground, and let loose the salty silver drops.

I hear a voice say, "I bet your first born I can limbo that there glistening fount and not get a drop on me."

Just beyond the arc of this here glistening fount comes the shadow of Katie's ex. The very sound must have summoned him to the scene. A djinn of the gutter, a connoisseur of unmasked moments, the happy bard's ears have led him right to the sort of grand entrance he's been waiting for all his life.

Standing there all nordic and lopsided, Adam Jostler folds his arms and gazes upon the erosion at ground zero. He's at least seven inches taller than me, plus another five in his Australian green cowboy hat. A rosewood guitar is slung across his back. Sparse sideburns trickle along his jaw beneath the needlepoints of his gallant mustache stabbing the joints of a bristling blonde beard.

"You got a lot in you, buddy," he says. "Been saving up for days, I bet. Saving for just this moment, I bet. It's the way you are, Mister Wagner.... What do you say— will you wager your progeny against the stability of your steaming parabola?"

Adam tips his hat and cracks his knuckles. I glance at him without a word. He sort of ducks his head like he's going to bend over. He pantomimes a slouch and says, "You don't mind if I—," and his next movement? Merely a grin. Not only true to his word, but lilting in a way—innocent and cartoonish and without a stumble, Adam crab-walks like a defective puppet to emerge dry as a pastor on the far side. Then he's up again, a whole new man facing the trash bin with arms outstretched for inspection.

"That's all she wrote," he says. "Say goodbye to the proudest pound of flesh your dangling participle could ever produce. You can visit on weekends. Look at you, still going strong! What endless well of life do you drag around down there?"

When I chuckle my body bounces, staggering the stream into leaflets of pee. My smile fades away. My piss diminishes, becoming a dribble. Folded away and zipped up.

"I'm never having kids," I tell him.

"That's what Katie used to say." Adam's smile takes on a maudlin nostalgia. "Have you seen her?"

"Yeah," I say.

"Is she okay?"

It breaks my heart not to tell him Katie's still a virgin, because it's clear he's worried about who the baby-daddy might be, and whether he even still has a chance with her at this point. They've been broken up a long time now, but who knows. They say a baby changes everything. I can't tell him there's no father, though, because I'm sworn to secrecy. Whether or not he thinks she cheated on him, it's pretty clear he's still in love with her. I'm sure Katie knows this. I think women always know, even if sometimes they say they don't. It's all tactics.

"She isn't dating anyone," I tell him.

"Oh, I know," he retreats. "It's not that. I'm just curious how she's holding up."

"She seems fine. She's about due."

He nods carefully, backing away from the topic. Then he strangles both sides of his belly with his huge hands and gives it an accordion squeeze. He looks up and says to me, "What about breakfast?"

"What about it?"

"Someone makes it. We eat it," says he. "Let's go before I die. Got any money?"

I fish around my pockets, but I already know the answer. Not even enough for toast. I continue to dig, fingers swirling the empty cloth like a turbine.

"It's okay," says Adam. "We've got friends all up and down Higgins. I know at least two people I can talk into owing me money."

2.

Missoula's population is small enough so everyone knows everyone, but large enough there's not enough time for everyone you know. Missoula is right in the annoying middle, population-wise. Like the awkward teenager version of a city. Katie Ludwick used to say, "You see so many people on the street you kinda-sorta know—or maybe met once or twice at a show—that if you stopped to talk to them all you'd never make it to where you're going." Dealing with this leads to the unspoken social convention of not acknowledging anyone until you know them *really* well. There've been times where I couldn't establish eye contact with the same person who told me their life story only a week before. On the other hand, I've found that a lot more people are willing to meet and have an honest conversation when they know they won't have to pay for it later with large chunks out of their schedule.

Adam has never worried about this sort of thing. He will meet you and be your friend and that's all there is to it.

His green overcoat sweeps his ankles. His spine is joyful and straight. A few years back he lost a canine and most of the tooth next to it when an SUV full of douchebags jumped him just for looking weird. This has no impact whatsoever on his ability to rejoice in almost anything that goes down. Adam is a career grinner. He smiles the way the rest of us breathe, and his smile is always genuine. It's a lot of hard work to smile that often with so much sincerity. Try it for a while and see if you have the energy left over to hold a real job.

We walk back toward the bridge, but instead of crossing, Adam leads us down the slope and into the park where we stand side-by-side staring over the river's vagrant flow.

Without looking away from the water, he reaches into his pocket and produces a half-bitten shell, holds it out to me. "Peanut?"

"For breakfast?"

He tosses the peanut into the current. It bobs and floats away like a message in a bottle.

"Let's swim," he says.

"They made that bridge for a reason," I say.

"A swim will wake you up."

"I've been awake for hours."

"I haven't," Adam argues. "Come on, it's warm. When's the last time you swam across the river?"

"Never. Isn't it seven years bad luck to swim before you eat?"

"That's after. Come on."

"What about your guitar?"

"Some hippie gave it to me. I'll leave it here for the next guy."

3.

Dean always used to say that if cell phones had hit the market ten years earlier, Katie Ludwick and Adam Jostler would never have fallen in love.

They first met right after Katie and Amelia got home from their big road trip around the U.S. They'd gutted-out an RC Cola van, insulated it with egg crates, and installed bunk beds in the back. They read *On the Road* while on the road and lived the Kerouac dream. I caught the tail end of their trip on my way back from India. We all met up in Pismo Beach. We wrapped Katie in seaweed and dragged her into the surf. We stole an American Flag. We drove a convertible the wrong way up the freeway ramp and fixed their van's broken stick shift with duct tape and spare pieces of home hardware. We got drunk and screamed at the sea and the stars to promise to keep up the good work. We spent an entire day in Wal-Mart taking pictures of items with a disposable camera we snatched off the shelves. Then we dropped the camera off at the Wal-Mart development station. Two hours later, we got the pictures back and placed each one next to its original subject. We left the store empty handed, then debated about whether what we'd done was stealing.

The entire time Katie Ludwick and Amelia's great American adventure was underway, they'd left their house in the care of another woman also named Katie. When they got back to Missoula, Katie Ludwick took over the house again and the other Katie found a place of her own. It just so happened that this other Katie was good friends with Adam Jostler; so one day, shortly after the other Katie moved out and our Katie moved back in, Adam called the house looking for the other Katie. He called using his friend's black rotary wall phone. Katie's orange rotary wall phone rang, and Amelia answered. Adam said, "Is Katie there?" and Amelia handed the phone to Katie Ludwick.

"It's Adam," Amelia said, thinking the call was for our Katie and not the other Katie. But our Katie had never met Adam Jostler. She did have a friend named Adam Nickerson, though, and she assumed it must be him on the line.

Because Katie was in a hurry that day, she and

Adam made quick plans to meet up, each thinking the other was someone else.

"Come down to Flippers in an hour. I'll be on the machines," Katie said, and hung up the phone.

When Adam arrived, Katie Ludwick was the only other person in the casino. Adam was about fifteen minutes late, so he walked up to her and said, "I'm looking for my friend Katie. Has anyone else been in here in the last half hour?"

Katie Ludwick looked up into the glow of the keno machine reflecting off his wide, gentle eyes and fell in love. Adam fell in love too, but for him it happened a few minutes later, when, following an awkward exchange of confused questions, both of them realized how the whole mix-up had gone down. Epiphanies collided and his heart did swoon.

The new couple found an apartment and moved in together the very next month. Adam paid his friend ten bucks for the phone he'd used to make that fortuitous call. Katie brought along her orange phone, and they set them side-by-side on the table and never plugged either one into the wall.

4.

Mid-winter, Missoula's Clark Fork River becomes a junkyard.

In the summer she is a highwater railroad of revenge, pulling down trees, fence posts, and the occasional angler. Then, after a raft of inner tube invasions, she dwindles and slows through autumn, before freezing into a slush mill of ice, driftwood, and the shavings of civilization. Twists of metal piping, rolls of chicken wire, a fallen telephone pole, an overturned couch upholstered in frost—all dry-docked in this dwindling whisper between encroaching banks of snow.

Right now she's in that calm, low and empty phase.

It's still warm enough we probably won't get hypothermia. I stare at the ghostly swirls and peel off my socks, while Adam strips down to nothing but.

I hold my right boot up by the heel.

"What about when we get across?"

He puts a foot in the water and crinkles up his nose. "Hm?"

"Our clothes."

"Oh."

Adam folds his hands over the top of his head. He faces me naked and deflating in the wind, furry belly flopping thoughtfully forward.

Then he dashes off, only to return with a large plastic grocery bag, into which he stuffs his clothes. As he stuffs, he glances my way as if giving a demonstration.

"Where'd you find that?" I ask.

"The trash behind Flippers. It's clean."

"We're going to get arrested."

"Okay, clothes go in bag. Bag goes on top of head. Like this."

"Okay."

"And I attach it to my head with the belt."

I watch him attempt this. He cinches it down with a notch to spare. I remove my hoodie. Adam balances the load. Off comes my shirt. Adam clasps the belt buckle under his chin as I unlatch my own, dropping my drawers in public for the second time in fifteen minutes. Adam's bag starts to slip. He steadies it with a hand, somehow advancing another notch on the belt.

His beard struts out in front of the leather strap like a fan. He dips a timid toe into the water.

I step out of my pants, and bundle all my clothes together as Adam kneels down, opening up his head to receive them. Everything fits but the hoodie. Something tells me that if I had my boxer's jacket, this wouldn't be a problem.

"Wrap it around your head," Adam says.

"Like this?"

"Okay. Let's go."

"I changed my mind. Give me my clothes."

"Too late."

"I'm serious."

"Jump in! All at once."

Two splashes off the bank. Kids lean over the bridge, dropping stones. Others fly by, coiled up in hot rods or on the skeleton spines of motorcycles, going as fast as they can in case the bridge decides to collapse. A trail meets the slope on the far shore where it bulges and relaxes into the spread of downtown.

We swim where we can, keeping our heads above water. The first few seconds near paralysis, but we splash around and adjust to the cold. Three college students float by on inner tubes. We try to keep swimming even in the shallows. It sucks to put feet down on the rocks of a river bottom; best to crawl along on fingertips instead. A few small islands block our path. Adam gets out and walks, but I swim around, refusing to leave the water until I can put my clothes back on. Halfway across, I remember what Amelia said about breaking the river. I try it with my fist. The splash recoils and gets me in right in the eye. Adam looks back and wants to know what I'm doing. "Nevermind," I say. Five minutes later we're both shivering on the farther shore.

"Gimme my pants," I demand, standing with naked arms wrapped around a naked chest, watering the grass beneath me.

"Boots. Shirt. You had two socks, right?"

"I'm freezing."

"Come on, technically it's still summer," he says. "How greasy do you want breakfast?"

I wrap, buckle, zip, button, lace. Adam wipes himself down with his jeans. Some ways off a family of four takes a walk through the park. The little boy points, and I flap hands at Adam to quicken up.

He says, "If you want maximum grease, the Oxford's our best bet. I have a hangover, so I vote maximum grease. What do you want to eat?"

"Toast."

"Greasy toast?"

I'm still flapping, looking over my shoulder for the cops. Adam sticks his hand down the throat of a sock and stretches cotton-webbed fingers to the sun. Makes a fist, pulls the insides out in one swift tug.

"Put your pants on first," I say.

"Love thy tootsies above all else. Think of what they do for you. Do you know the foot has more natural curves per square inch than any other part of the body? What could be more provocative than bare feet?"

Last of all, Adam buffs his beard. He shakes and wrings and brushes until dry. Satisfied, he slaps his legs.

"Okay?"

"Breakfast."

"Grease?"

"Toast."

Las Vegas, NV

"THANKS FOR BEING THERE WHEN I need you," she used to say, "and for not being there when I don't."

We liked to sit on the grass under a fig tree by the pond in a park under the glow of Las Vegas lights, wrapped in the smell of a campfire, leaning out over a skywalk, trying to come across as clever, sincere, mysterious, wanton, aloof, desperate, insatiable, cool, easy, injured, vibrant, independent, eternally devoted.

I carved our initials into some wood. This is actually something people do.

"Mr. Wagner," she said, "—are you in love with me?"

"I'm under love with you," I said. I didn't want to give away the game. "Just barely below the love line, the boiling point between love and not-quite-love. I'm right under that."

"So watch my step is what you're saying."

When I pulled her toward me she fit perfectly in the awkward jutting curve-free jabby rib cage part of my right flank.

Sometimes I scared her. I lost my shit, tore out my hair, punched a wall, smashed a violin, panicked and trembled like a baby, grew distant, climbed out of bed at 3am to walk through still-sweltering streets, contemplated suicide, withdrew emotionally, refused to say what I was thinking.

"Yoshie, let's live on a sailboat."

We liked to go people watching. In malls, bars, casinos, theaters. Once we tried going to a theater to watch the audience instead of the show. Train stations were her favorite. Reunions and good-byes. "How many are falling in love, or thinking about divorce, lying to each other, pregnant and don't know it yet, developing cancer, hours away from a car crash..."

At home I dodged the heat by lying on the living room floor, eyes closed. Sometimes she'd crawl over and sing to me. Inches from my ear. Some raspy blue melody that made me hallucinate black-and-white images. Dark clouds with white glowing edges. Fields of grey grass. A silver carafe, empty. Vegas in the 20s. A tall peak and a distant gulf growing ever wider and rushing toward me at the same time.

"About the sailboat," she said, "I changed my mind."

This is actually something people do.

5.

Adam and I pass through Caras park, where brass sculptures of fish perch on grassy tumors and the trail becomes a stone wall toppling toward the river. In the middle a pavilion waits on concerts, festivals, impromptu pagan holidays, and farmers' markets—as well as drug deals, games of human chess, and the occasional street musician.

"I have to stop here," Adam says, standing in front of white bricks and a revolving door.

"What for?"

"I have to go in. I'll just be a minute."

He folds his hands behind his back. Hops up and down like he's trying to see through one of the upper windows. "Wait here."

"Okay."

I'm left alone with my thoughts, gazing down the sidewalk toward the place where the bridge crests its own horizon. A bicycle rolls by, and sinks beyond the summit. I wiggle my fingers. "Zozezaz," I say. A small cloud swims behind the Wilma Theater and is gone. "Zozezaz!" Predictable paths lead toward vanishing points. I feel better pretending to control them all. A bird flies under the bridge—*Zozezaz*—and never returns. Everything on its way out. What would be the last thing to go out of the dregs of a dissolving world? And would that last thing be able to follow, surrounded by nothing at all, with nowhere even left to vanish to?

In much the same way, Vegas Girl curled up and disappeared from my life.

But there was this one moment lying in bed, long before the end, when I could see it coming, when I knew she was going to leave me.

"Yoshie," she said. "I want ice cream."

Wearing only a bathrobe, I drove her little red Mazda down to the grocery store. A comfy purple bathrobe. Nothing underneath. The night was hot.

If this had been a book or a movie, a cop would have pulled me over, but I drove with care.

I wanted something dramatic to happen so I could write a story about it. Maybe I'd get mugged on my way across the parking lot, then rip open the robe and flash the bastard, sending him screaming into the wild Vegas streets. But it was just another moment in a wide net of moments. I guess I'd reached the age where I could walk out into the world naked but for a bathrobe and nothing weird was going to happen to me.

I picked up ice cream and brought it back, and she slurped it down with no expression. Watching the light of the TV dance in her unblinking eyes, I realized how much better it is to want something than to get it. Longing is life. Possession binds you to the ground. I watched the ice cream melt all desire out of her sweet face and I knew right then we couldn't last. For about thirty seconds it didn't matter. In that brief window of time she could have turned to me, touched my hand, told me it was over—that she was leaving forever—and it wouldn't have hurt at all.

By the time we ended for reals, such thoughts had become impossible. There are minutes, holes in the continuum, when disappointment can be the best thing in the world. Then perspective rushes away, and men become fragile as kindling once more.

Adam returns to me on the sidewalk. He snaps a dollar bill in front of my face.

"Have you seen this man?"

"How much did you get?"

"Maybe three dollars. Coffee, toast and a side of grease. I want hash browns."

"We don't have enough."

"Swim felt good, don't you think?" Adam takes off his shirt again, balls it up and dries his armpits. He puts his thumbs up to his breast as if seeking suspenders to snap. He leans back on his heels and laughs. "A king's table awaits us at the Oxford."

6.

The Oxford Diner plays metronome for Missoula's oldtown strip. Starting out in 1883 as a small grill in a teepee down by the river, the Ox moved to Broadway in the 50s and then to its final resting place on the corner of Higgins and Pine.

Photographs, postcards, and portraits watch over us from the Oxford's walls, telling Missoula's story in black and white—smudged and water-damaged with curled corners and insignificant signatures. The legacy of foundational regulars, I assume. Former patrons, bartenders and cooks, cyclical hobos, good American pioneers, hard workers (or at the very least hard at work avoiding work), and the wrinkled mugs of old men from heavy northwestern railroad. Frame after frame of tilted heads, squinty eyes, layers of skin folded like peaks and troughs in the stock market. What souls rushed along the highways and canyons of those wrinkles?

At the Ox you pay before they feed you. Once we settle up, our waitress brings out toast and hash browns and gravy and coffee and apple juice all floating on one gigantic platter. I start in on the toast, scraping grape jelly waves over crusty shores. Adam doesn't touch his food. Says he wants to let the grease settle. He pulls out a pack of rolling papers, slips one loose and holds it out like he's offering a tissue.

"You want?"

"I quit."

"Me too," Adam says.

He places a pinch of fresh tobacco in the middle of the paper and flattens it down with his fingertip.

I watch him rub the two sides of the rollie together, up and down. He licks one edge. He does it by keeping his tongue in place and sliding the paper across with both hands, right to left like a platen cylinder. Seals it into a cone-shaped stub and tucks it behind his ear.

"You did, huh?" I leer with suspicion.

"Yep. This is just in case."

"In case you start again?"

Adam shoves a spoon into his breakfast. "I'm addicted to rolling them."

"There's no Tabasco sauce."

"I made a deal with the Devil," he says. "I am dying from the cancers, I told him. Help me quit smoking and I'll do anything, I told him. Do you know what the Devil said?" Adam hands me a bottle.

"This is green."

"You've never had green Tabasco?"

"Seriously?"

"I used to take shots of this stuff. Try it. It's good. Anyway, the Devil tells me he will cure my addiction, but there must be a trade! For Satan does not have the power to create or destroy, only to sift."

"Sift?"

"Only to sift," he says. "No longer would I crave the smoke in my lungs, but from then on I'd be addicted to the act of rolling. And so it goes. Conservation of addiction. One way or another, I'm still hooked."

I rub my eyes, remembering my love for the Oxford like the secret blissful terror of psychedelics and roller coasters. That common thread of familiar suspicion and permissive creepiness developing through any series of myth, madness, and in fact nostalgia—each of which has a forever hand in seasoning Oxford evenings. *Brains and Eggs* still on the menu and all is right with the world. It's the unabashed gutteresquity that draws us here. No deceit in the Oxford, no double-faced pleasantry. Everyone from bankers to preachers to millwrights to students to senators can be at their comfortable wormiest. Outrageous behavior might breed a delicacy of violence, but no one ever got a knife in the back. Not yet anyway. Curses, insults, and respectful fist fights weave a counterintuitive grid of relative security over those who pass through the Oxford's jingling door.

Adam says, "So about Katie," as I shovel up a mouthful of hashed browns dripping green. "I haven't seen her since she kicked me out."

"Pretty weird for this town."

"Should I talk to her?"

"Do you want to talk to her?"

He stares me in the eye and the stare says: *She cheated on me, Josh.* But my counter-stare says, *No she didn't, you dumbass.* He doesn't catch on. He probably thinks my eyes are saying, *Yes, you're quite the chump, aren't you?*

He holds a piece of toast out in front of his face, looking more like a little boy than ever before.

"Can I tell you something?" he says.

"Sure."

"I haven't told anyone this, and it's driving me crazy. I think I can trust you with the secret."

"Okay."

"I want her back," he says.

"That's a secret?"

There are these tiny, succulent moments when I can render Adam speechless that I wouldn't trade for anything.

"Everybody knows," I continue, "I'm pretty sure even Katie knows."

"That obvious?"

"Look," I tell him. "She hasn't dated anyone since you guys broke up. Why not tell her how you feel? Go nuts."

"I don't know."

"It's what you're supposed to do," I say.

"Maybe I should wait. Until after she has the baby."

"Just tell her. If she wants you back, why wait any longer?"

His eyes go wide around a spoonful of grease. "What if she doesn't want me back?"

"Then get rejected already so you can stop worrying about it."

"You think she'll reject me?"

"It is impossible to predict anything when it comes to women. It's all darts and blindfolds."

7.

But Adam no longer pays attention to me. Howls rise from the far side of the room. Chairs hit the floor. Five guys in a horseshoe formation stumble in. Five guys with a single note of laughter passed between them, resonating throughout the chamber of their conjoined bodies.

Adam tilts an eyebrow and glances over my shoulder. His follow-up gesture indicates something I can't decipher. One of the five—a heavy, lumbering guy whose baby face kind of floats out ahead of the onslaught—spots us and points, directing his laughter our way, focusing it through a pair of lip rings.

"Hey!"

"Hey!"

"Hey!"

"Hey!"

Which is all still laughter, trying to take on the form of language—as if laughter itself was not language.

Adam smacks their names through dribbling lips of gravy, and I can't understand a word.

The pointing guy rubs his bowling ball head with a deck of meaty fingers.

"Adam has a cigarette," he shouts.

Oh?

All five seem to leap the length of the Oxford floor. They surround Adam, tackling him, groping toward him all at once. Adam dodges, presents the palm of his hand just in time to catch a face. Teeth gnash and a playful growl rises up as they tear at him like a pack of plush dogs.

Which is all still laughter, trying to take on the form of violence—as if laughter itself was not violence.

"Okay, okay! Just ask, okay? Ow!"

The skinniest of the five, long sandy hair knotted up, glasses twisted, whose teeth have frozen against Adam's shoulder, without moving his jaw seems to say —*Can I have?*

The cigarette, dislodged from behind Adam's ear and now held tightly in his fist, is slowly revealed, inducing mock gasps of surprise and awe. Somehow the cigarette survives the attack unharmed. Not so Adam's hair, which he pampers before setting out four new rolls.

"I need more room!"

The five lead Adam to the last open table in the joint. They perch around his left shoulder as he hunches over his work.

But I'm not completely abandoned. Another man, a tagalong to the five—fella in his late fifties—somehow ends up with the original cigarette. He lights it and falls into the chair across from me, scratching an ear and tugging his short, grey beard.

"What was I saying?" he asks.

"Nothing," I tell him.

He crosses his arms and leans forward with tiny eyes, like a bird's, peering over the top of his glasses and into mine. I have never felt so much a part of a telepathic conversation. He savors his smoke, exhaling against a tall blue dimpled plastic glass of water. Words follow, emerging from the fog, spilling across the table.

"I remember I was dreaming. And I remember knowing I was dreaming. And it was raining, or it had been. In the dream it was just after a rain. I was looking at my glasses, holding them up. There were little flat drops all over the lenses. And I remember one drop making a slow, jagged trail. And now I can't remember if it was on the outside or inside of the lens. I kept thinking how amazing it was that I was dreaming and looking at it, and that I knew I was dreaming. That my brain could create this kind of detail. For itself. To create it and look at it and be amazed by it all at once."

Behind the man, the Oxford's back door opens, admitting a puff of wind. I can see the rectangle of daylight wrap around the head of my new companion, as all the leftover darkness shoves inward and onto his face.

"What was I saying?"

I set my toast down, pick it up again and nibble the crust. "You were dreaming," For a second he looks like a rubber toy, like I should squeeze him.

"Rain," I amend, tucking my hands under my thighs.

"Rain," the man repeats, drawing the word out and burying it in a cloud of smoke.

8.

OVER BY THE BACK DOOR a man in a Cubs cap and white jacket has just walked in. Sort of a doughy face pimpled with bright blue eyes. There's a name tag on his jacket, but I can't read it. He leans down and picks up two wooden crates, then turns back toward the door, waddling with a crate under each arm.

A waitress rushes him. Head waitress from the look of it. She wears a black hair net. Her face is painted on. Her fingers stab outward like iron webbing. "Excuse me! Excuse me!" She's spitting on the man, on purpose or not, all just coming out with her words.

The man turns to face her and says, "Listen. Listen. Listen," which is exactly what she refuses to do. The man bobs the crates up and down, a failed attempt at hypnosis.

The waitress' spine is bent in at least five places. Her bones must be wires. Her skin sags in folds and pouches. She continues spitting. "You can't take those. No. You cannot. Take those. Who do you think you are?"

"This is my job, lady. You want to see the paperwork?"

From the other table, I hear Adam cough and snort. Four of the five now stand in a row opposite him, leaning against a single chair. The fifth, in torn jeans and long black jacket, a pair of red razor stripes racing down his neck, crouches at the end of the table, locked in the tunnel of his sideburns. He gives Adam a nudge and Adam hands over a cigarette.

The man sitting across from me says, "A raindrop crawling down the lens, leaving streaks like frozen lightning."

"Who the hell do you think you are?" the waitress screams. "Put those crates down right now, goddammit or I'll have you hauled away."

"Look. Look at the paper, lady."

"Have *you* hauled away."

"Look at the words." Still clutching the crates, the man holds out a pink carbon receipt.

Her hands go straight to her hips—her eyes nowhere near his papers. Curses tangle, marbling in her mouth. She's trembling, her face defiant. Other waitresses inch near, hesitant, glancing at each other for guidance.

"You don't open this door. Not without knocking." She's no longer screaming. Retired words reduced to a choked futility. "You don't take these crates. You can take your paperwork right back to your boss and have him shove it up his hole."

Most of the customers barely notice, lost in their isolated worlds. One, maybe two glances up and down. I've never felt so disjointed, so disconnected with everything. There was a time I remember the world made sense, when it felt cohesive. Now there are only splinters and fragments.

I look to Adam, still huddled in mid-roll. His shoulders rowing. The five suck down their smokes, pantomiming a riot, eyes glowing bright for the duration of each drag, cheeks pulled tight. But only the man in front of me ever exhales. Exhaling the smoke that the others breathe in.

The crate man says, "It's just my job, okay? Like you have a job, I have a job. I have to take these—listen, calm down. I have to take these crates. I have to—"

The old man tells me: "Background in a mist. I remember thinking this was Japan in the early morning."

I've already forgotten what he was trying to say.

"I was too focused on the drop," he says. "I couldn't see the background. It blurred past my perception, like an oil painting, water-damaged, curled up and bending over my back."

"The raindrop?"

"The world."

Adam is tossing cigarettes now—one, two, three, four—into the open mouths of his patrons, who swallow them whole and beg for more. I can hear him pinching and licking and handing over. The five smoke faster than he can roll. All conversation long faded away. No time for it. Dive straight for the source. Their addictions play off one another, a perpetual fever derailed from the track of time. A man shoveling dirt into the air.

Somewhere between desire and contentment there are tiny fractures, cracks of panic. Moments where continuity is lost and reason cannot find it again. Isolated space dissected from the threads of reality, where passion emerges spontaneously and something finds the freedom to arise from nothing.

The waitress in tears.

"Get out of my bar."

The man in the white coat unmoved.

"I have papers. Papers say that I can take these."

"Never come back. Never come back here."

It's about the closest he'll ever get to permission, so he goes for the door. But at the last instant the waitress shudders, twists and flails her arms as if breaking loose from her own elbows. She groans and tears at him with hands and nails and spit, knocking one of the crates out from under his arm.

It hits the ground, corner first. Splinters fly. Conversations pause, skipping like a scratch on a record, then, realizing all the fuss is only a crate, continue. I see myself broken into wooden bits, lying on the kitchen floors of a hundred diners across America.

When I stand up, the old man across from me doesn't seem to notice. He stares at my belt and says, "The drop reflected everything, just like a real drop. Such detail. Such precision. Such clarity of thought."

Chips of wood. The waitress sobbing. Her face open flat like a ledger on a pedestal of hands.

I need to get out of here, I think. Though not in so many words.

The man in the white coat hustles out the back door, trying to appear as if he's just passing on through. One crate under his arm.

I check to see if Adam is still rolling. His shoulders whir like hummingbird wings. A cloud of smoke hovers over the table like a thunderhead—heavy, ready to burst into rain at any moment, to extinguish its source.

A young waitress walks out from behind the bar with a broom in one hand, creeping up on the pile of splinters. Others gather around the head waitress, consoling, fingertips touching shoulders.

As I reach for the door it opens ahead of me. Amelia is there. She might as well be wrapped in a bow.

"Mister Wagner," she laughs. And then she really laughs, doubling over.

What's so funny?

"Come out here with me at once!"

CHAPTER FOUR

BROKEN

Denver, CO

NINETEEN IS MY RECORD for breakups with the
same woman. She was a beautiful Chippewa with
licorice hair and a kiss so soft you only felt the lump in
your throat. We first met in New Orleans, and then
again randomly in San Francisco, but mostly we hung
out in Denver. We'd breakup and get back together
again like a circadian rhythm. She was better at the
breaking up part, instigating thirteen of them, while I
can only take credit for five. The getting back together
was more-or-less down the middle. Our fifteenth
breakup was the most painful. The eighth was pretty
hilarious, I guess, looking back. Breakups four and five
could be seen as two sides of the same breakup, but

I'm still calling them separate. The first one was just stupid, and neither of us really understood why it went down. I remember eighteen staring out over a red canyon with high tide rising at my back. I have no memory of breakup nineteen. I just know it must've happened.

Sometimes it takes nineteen breakups to do the trick. Sometimes a thing has to be broken over and over again before it can be fixed for good.

Some love goes away. Some love never goes away. You have to go away from love before you can find out if love ever plans on going away from you. But if you stray too far, lingering love can become a haunting thing. It influences every dream. It hides under the fingernails of each decision. You may have gone away from it, but it stays with you, clinging to your shoulders, and the road back feels a hundred times longer. It becomes burdensome, not because of the love, but because of the road. The road presses up on the feet of the traveler haunted by love.

There are exes you can see again, go out drinking with, flirt and laugh with. There are exes you can meet on a lonely evening for a fuck and a smoke. And there are exes with whom it is too dangerous to allow even a moment's eye contact. These are not exes at all, and never will be, and that's the problem.

1.

Back on Amelia's arm, I'm pulled toward the fulcrum of the bridge. We sway as we walk, and Amelia's sprightly mannerisms slowly untangle the Oxford's lingering mood.

"What did you do today?" she asks.

"I hate that question," I say.

"Don't be a prick. Just tell me."

"Aren't we a little past small-talk?"

Amelia cracks the knuckles in her left hand. "Boys are very stupid. Small talk is the overture to big talk. You can't just dive directly into a deep conversation."

"Why not?"

"Because everything needs a reference. Everything

evolves from a simpler entity. From something small and trivial. Trees grow from seeds. Chickens from eggs. Meaning develops over time."

"This conversation got deep pretty fast."

"Yes, because you and I are well practiced. But it wouldn't have happened at all if I hadn't asked about your day."

We head west as the sun kneels on the horizon. The river flows toward us beneath a canopy of wires sprouting from two lanes of splintering telephone poles. When we've all upgraded to smartphones and brain implants, will this legacy of giants remain? There must be millions of them in the United States alone, clustered in neighborhoods and stretched out across the plains like totems of information.

Amelia says, "How was the Oxford?"

"A waitress freaked out over some crates."

"Typical." She pauses to straighten her tights.

"Adam was there."

"Oh yes! How is he?"

"Brokenhearted."

"He loves her," she says.

"He'd make a great dad if he could get his shit together."

Amelia nods. "And probably even if he can't."

"Maybe he really is the father."

"There is no father," she says.

"You believe that?"

"When was the last time Katie lied about anything?"

She has me there. I can do nothing but change the subject. I ask, "And how many boys are pining over you these days?"

"A few." Amelia's rubs her hands together like a mad-scientist. "My dating habits resemble solar systems. There is always one guy who is the sun, and then there are the planets, and occasionally I flirt with satellites. Now and then I make out with an asteroid belt. But if I were to commit and only date the sun, I would become bored and drift away. The poor men I date for no other reason than to keep some other man at the precise distance where dating him remains possible."

I'm not surprised to learn a woman as complex as Amelia requires high-level mathematical formulas to navigate her relationships.

"The real question is, who's been breaking your heart, Mister Wagner?"

"We break our own hearts."

"Oh?"

"Love is the universe striking two stones over and over until there's a spark. It isn't something anyone does. Who is qualified to judge? How can there be any real blame in there anywhere?"

Amelia thinks it over, not quite following.

"Okay, it's like this," I say. "You and I are friends. I could go weeks without calling you and it wouldn't make a difference. But when love steps in, even a couple days of silence can cause a dent. If we're friends and I stand you up for a date it might be annoying, but if we're in love and I stand you up, it's devastating."

"Same behavior. Two effects."

"Right. So instead of saying so-and-so broke my heart, it should be: I have broken my heart against you."

She tries out the phrase, "I broke my heart against your heart." Then she takes my arm. "Come on."

"Where are we going?" I ask.

"To gather the masses," she says.

2.

We weave a drunken saw-tooth through Missoula until dusk, absorbing stragglers along the way. One or two at a time, until our gang resembles a class of grade-schoolers on a field trip. We run into Freedom and Megan skipping down the sidewalk; Jake, Slink, and Beatrice around the corner from Missoula's giant Bill the Cat statue; Margie and Jan and Barb and Paul tumble out of a casino. As soon as our ranks surpass a dozen, Amelia springs her plan.

"There's a party at Katie's house," she says.

"Does Katie know about this?"

"Certainly not."

"When does it start?"

"As soon as we arrive."

What a fisher of men is Amelia Tigerheart.

More! We need more. It becomes a game to see how many humans we can gather. We are the Great Attractor, a multiplying, morphing mob of merriment.

Butterfly Herbs is our first filling station. Tucked into the main strip of downtown, Butterfly is an apothecary, a coffee shop, a deli, and the sipping, sniping, doodling, riotous center of Missoula's renegade arts community. Everyone who works at Butterfly Herbs doubles as a regular. It's hard to tell when someone is on the clock or not. Baristas flow from countertop collaborations to booth-side hugs to the back alley for a smoke, while customers hop up to get their own coffee, or go back to the cooler for extra cream.

They're all artists or writers or musicians or aspiring filmmakers or old rainbow festival shaman-in-training-types or young hitchhiking tribal punks with bright green eyes and crooked yellow teeth, wrapped in hand-stitched puzzles of patch, earth tones, rainbows, scarves, buttons, tatters and thread. The backs of most of their hands are smudged in black or red stamps from the night before. In Missoula everyone knows everyone, but in Butterfly, everyone knows everyone's story. A basketful of peers, friends, and lovers—the blazing youth of the northwest, unconcerned and unaware of how quickly they are rushing into the future. Spirits of the earth. Here they gather for inspiration, conversation, caffeine, and mutual hangover recovery sessions.

I soak in the sight—these emerging spirits who dress like travelers, drink like rock stars, converse like debutante savants, cuss like rednecks, fight like assholes, and love like hippies. I am in awe of each and every one of them.

Alice, wearing a coat made entirely out of neckties, raises her hand like a first grader with a fierce longing for recess. Her eyebrows bounce over blue horn-rimmed gramma glasses, and her grin bursts at its edges. "I will call some people who know people and they'll tell some bands who know bands to come and play."

Sitting beside her is Mark, ever snug in vest, double Windsor, and patchwork pants, combing through his wiry Rasputin beard. His mascara wears thin. His head crests the top of my shoulder. Mark can reference Sam Keith, Dorothy Parker, and Georges Bataille in the same sentence with no accident of accuracy.

"How do you always look so sharp?" I ask him.

"Victorian England is my guide. Men have forgotten how to dress. Cuff links," he points to his wrists, "for instance."

Len, sitting across from him, chuckles into his coffee. Always composed, Len is the proud owner of the most Cheshire grin west of the Divide. He always pauses to think before speaking, and when he finally says something it tends toward aphorism. Like it's his job to run around tying up loose conversations. He is sandwiched between Carissa on one side (perpetually fourteen, incorruptible sprite), and Jayne on the other (voracious gobbler of drugs and juggler of beats), who plays chess with Watson, an artist of quiet composition (99% satyr, 1% stone).

Back out on Higgins, our pilgrimage nears thirty souls. The hours have fled and the mountains have slurped up the sun. We meander into the Wilma, the Howards, then down East Front Street, stopping now-and-again to get a different kind of high in every home. No one is ever quite ready to go when we arrive. We become a great pestering thing, an amorphous orrery, tethered by the occult affection of inside-jokes. Be thou assimilated! Share our flasks and tobacco. Interlocking arms, elbows hugflung neck to chin, passing one another from shoulder to shoulder. We invade living rooms, spill onto back porches, and scale rooftops.

We are pawns to the vibrations of stars, united until our final destination. Then, with splash of dish soap, our oily cabal fractures. We split into triplets, couplets, and singlets to re-merge with friends who have preceded us, all in a surge through Katie Ludwick's front door, our clan of forty-nine.

3.

BUT KATIE IS NOT YET home to witness the flood. Some pounce upon the stereo, others start to cook. We empty her fridge to make room for beer.

Amelia swings her arms wide and spins in circles. "I'm going to dance. But first, I'm going to smoke."

We linger on the porch. I slump down on the ripped-out backseat of an 80s van. Amelia perches in an orange barber's chair vintage enough for chrome ashtrays in the arm rests. The porch is trimmed with kettles and woks, with sleeping bags, hammocks, and bicycle tires.

Amelia exhales a curtain of smoke. As it parts, she orders me to tell her more about the woman I tried to marry.

"Vegas Girl?"

"Unless there's another one."

"What's to tell? We broke up. Kind of."

"Kind of a little bit?"

I think it over, but it's just the wishful kind.

"No. Kind of entirely."

Amelia investigates my eyes.

"So. She's down there and you're up here, and you're pretty sure it's over but you aren't exactly ready for it to be."

"Something like that."

Her fingers touch the hem of my shirt. "I'm going to tell you a secret. Are you ready?"

"What secret?"

"You're happy."

I snort cynicism. "Uh, no. I'm fucking miserable."

"Did she cheat on you? Did she tell you she needs 'space'?"

"I can't even begin to describe It."

She touches my arm. "See, that's love. You're happy. You just don't know it. You probably won't know it until it's too late, but right now—this moment—this is the happiest moment of your life. And if you're very lucky, you'll realize it for a split second and that split second will get burned into your brain and you'll remember it later on when everything is actual shit, and the memory will be what it takes to keep you going."

"I don't think so," I object. "I've been happy before, I know what it feels like, and it doesn't feel like this."

"You have no idea what happiness feels like," Amelia says. "You remember some sort of chemical-overload from the moments when everything was going your happy-go-lucky way. Remember? Tra-la-la! Birds and meadows. But that was not happiness. That was a trance you lived through. That was electroshock therapy. This? This right here—holding your guts in your hand—this is happiness."

"Well, then happiness sucks."

"But it still does what it's supposed to. Do you want her back?"

I shrug. "Most of me does."

Amelia regains her drill-sergeant posture. "Then you must go back down and apologize at once."

"Apologize?"

"That's right."

"Um..."

She leans forward in the barber chair and wags a finger in my face. "Don't try to figure out who's to blame. When you're done expressing your anger—which is what I suppose coming back to Montana was all about—your next move is to apologize. Immediately."

"That's unfair."

"That's love."

"Is this like your small-talk thing?"

"Yes. There are lots of rituals involved when it comes to women. And there are dance steps, and there is body language, and none of it has to do with anything, but it is all there to facilitate the passage of time. The passage of time is key."

"I think I give up."

"That's a good start." She smashes her cigarette into the protruding half-moon ashtray on the barber chair armrest and throws her feet to the floor. "Let's go," she says. "I hear music."

4.

A band plays homemade instruments in Katie Ludwick's back yard beside a fire pit of blackened stones. Tonight the kids dress like grandparents. Accordions and banjos cling to threadbare suspenders. Pink octagon glasses and civil war caps. Flannel scarves and Balkan mustaches. We're just babies in thick glasses, plain cotton dresses, aprons, and a slight curl to our hair. Reincarnations of distant ancestors, our inheritance stolen from second-hand stores. We have no clue what we're doing.

I close my eyes to the accordion drone as firelight flickers like a crime scene. I indulge in the desperation of trying to catch the moment in words, but the holes in my language-net are gaping and moments are so very small.

A goat walks by. Two little horns. Grey beard. Chewing on something. This almost surprises me.

"What's with the goat?"

"It's a party goat," someone says. "It loves beer."

"Whose is it?"

"Dunno. I think it's a rental."

Amelia and I dance for a while, but I soon get bored and go inside to see if Katie's back. We're all dying to find out how she reacts to the shindig. We can call it a baby shower if we must.

"Ahoy, varmint!" Dean cries from within. His voice is loud, plush, and belligerent, slowing down all other sounds in the room. Adam stands beside him, grinning the grin of the great gray goose. I notice his eyes scanning the room for some sign of Katie Ludwick.

"She's not here yet," I tell him.

"Come drink of the whiskey!" Dean leaps toward me in three lumbering steps. He seems uncharacteristically energized. In moments like these I forget how tenuous his grip on reality can be, how a shift in the breeze can elevate stray delusions to overpowering debilitation. I am glad he's here, focused on the moment and not brooding over his ex-wife or the innumerable conspiracies lying dormant in his subconscious.

"Where's Will?"

"Developing some sort of neural network or something on his computer," Dean says.

We are bloodhounds moving through the kitchen. Adam digs beer bottles from molehills of ice.

"You forgot the jacket again," I say, scowling.

"What jacket?" Dean mumbles.

"The blue boxers jacket you gave me. I need it."

"You don't need it."

"I want it."

"Well, why didn't you say so?"

"I did!"

"I haven't seen that jacket in months. I think Katie has it."

Seattle, WA

Ages ago, when I was watching a friend's house for a few months in Seattle, I got stuck inside a woman. And by that I mean exactly what you think I mean. Stuck. Inside her. She apparently had some sort of medical condition of which relentless contractions were a rare reaction. We stopped. She blushed. I didn't move. I offered a quizzical glance in lieu of having the wherewithal to say anything whatsoever. "This has happened before," she said. "It could last for up to an hour, but in a minute you'll, you know, shrink down, and everything will be fine." But I didn't, and it wasn't. The pressure, and perhaps the novelty, kind of turned me on more. I expanded; she contracted.

Annoyed, she told me to think about baseball or something. Then, after an awkward moment, she slapped me in the face. I guess she hoped the shock would wither me. Again, opposite effect. I remember thinking that if this went on, I might end up prying her apart, working her down, breaking her resolve.

"We could be here for a while," she said.

There are giant beetles in South Africa who crush empty beer cans with their pincers. They'll happen across an old bud light in the desert and grab hold of it with pincers as long as their abdomens—and they'll crush it. Sometimes they crush it twenty or twenty-five times. They do this to dust their pincers with flecks of aluminum. Then they'll go off and show female beetles how shiny their pincers are, and the females get all weak in their beetle knees.

The Ceratoid anglerfish is a deep-sea monster with goblin jaws and teeth like icicles. This fish wins some galactic award for the number one screwball mating practice.

It goes down like so:

Female anglers will grow to over five feet long, but the males are only about the size of your fist. The males sniff their way over to the females. When a boy angler finds a lady angler, he takes his baby goblin jaws and bites down on her ass. He doesn't let go, first because his saliva fuses his lips to her skin, but more importantly because as soon as male anglerfish are born, their digestive systems break down and they start to disintegrate. The only way the male anglerfish can stay alive is by feeding off a female, grabbing on and never letting go.

So now this crazed anglerfish, literally love-starved, dangles off his girlfriend's booty like a dead pit bull. He has become a parasite. An extension of her circulatory system. He sucks nutrients from her body while she swims around minding her own business. But it's never enough, because even though he's slowed down the process, the male's body continues to dissolve. His eyes drop out of his head. He atrophies and falls to pieces until there's nothing left but a pair of fish balls, which, in one last gasp, explode into a cloud of sperm fertilizing the female's eggs.

And then there's fig wasps, who go at it before they're even born. Mating is the first rite of passage to existence. If you don't mate, you don't get to live.

Banana slugs are hermaphrodites who devour each other's penises in the name of love.

Or those little jumping spiders who look like they're teleporting everywhere. Once a year the mandibles of all the males swell up so they can't eat. They go mad with hunger and start thronging together into one big mosh-pit of death, killing the fuck out of each other. They do this on top of the females. Hundreds of them. In their death throes they unload all over the ladies, setting the stage for the next generation battle royale.

A significant percentage of animal sperm cells are useless for fertilization. These aggressive sperms accompany the creative sperms like bodyguards—assassins that hunt down and kill the sperm of competing males.

The next time I saw Seattle Girl a few years had gone by. She'd had a child. It didn't bother me at all to think of her with other men, only to picture her giving anyone else that bashful gaze and clinical apology. Or that slap in the face.

It was the first time any ex of mine had reproduced. Good eye contact that kid, steep gaze. And me thinking, "I could've been your daddy if she'd never let go."

Love is a virus we spread by breaking up with people. When you call it quits and leave someone, and when they go out and catch another, who falls for them and gets hurt, and then they go out and do the same and on and on and on... you take part in the great continuity of broken hearts. There's no first cause. And when an ex becomes a mom or a dad, you feel a little bit to blame, like if you had never broken up, then that particular child would never have been born.

How many babies are we fractionally responsible for? Think eight or nine layers down the tree, from breaker-uper to ninth-generation break-up-ee. How many of the spawn of exes and exes-of-exes could trace a thread back to any single link in our propagation of this love, this virus, that we spread by breaking up with people? How many fragments of baby do I have floating around out there? At least three by now that I know of, but the line goes deep, and the chain is long and complicated. Could be dozens. Hundreds.

The virus of love is spread through the subconscious. Side effects include increased heart rate, insomnia, euphoria, visions, nightmares, altered personality, erratic behavior, depression, rage, and babies.

Babies everywhere.

With sea horses, it's the males who carry and bear the young.

Most reef fish females will take a turn being male at some point in their life.

Japanese scientists have used parthenogenesis to create fatherless mice.

Of all the bizarre accounts of this phenomenon, including the case of Katie Ludwick, the weirdest by far happens all the time in the insect world. The culprit of this condition is not genetic, but bacterial. The Wolbachia pipientis is a bacterium that lives in the sex organs of around 15% of all insect species. Since the Wolbachia can only be transmitted from host mother to host child, these bacteria have adopted strategies for limiting the number of pesky male offspring useless to their cause. Like mad alchemists, the Wolbachia sometimes mess with the insects' hormones and change their male hosts into females. In other cases, the bacteria stops productive mating or eliminates the males of a population altogether, and parthenogenesis takes over as a last resort in maintaining the species.

Virgin pregnancy is nature's Hail Mary.

We understood this intuitively long before science confirmed the reality. From folktales and footnotes to Hellenic festival, and finally a cornerstone of the western church, the ripened virgin represents hope for the empty who long to be fulfilled, as well as the overfull tormented by a need for purgation.

And a child conceived spontaneously—such as Katie Ludwick's—occurs to us as both stillborn and immortal.

5.

THE HOURS PALE BY. THIS is the darkest before the dawn. Eight or nine new stragglers show up to replace those we've lost. They bring cases of beer, quarts of liquor, little curled-over baggies and aluminum squares of whatever. Nicotine light burns through every window, and from the parking lot Katie's building resembles a zoetrope moored in the dark.

As soon as everyone's good and loaded, Dean produces an old wooden pickax from God-knows-where, and starts screaming for the fucking laptops. No one knows what he's talking about, and we all assume he's just being Dean. But there really are laptops, and Katie arrives about fifteen minutes later to prove it. I could give a good goddamn about some old busted laptops, however, for Katie Ludwick is wearing my jacket.

"It's my jacket," she says.

"Okay, it's your jacket. Can I have it?"

"What's going on?"

"We threw a party."

"I can see that," she says.

"Your note said do what I want."

She gives me a long, smoldering stare that masks her secret delight. She says, "You can have the jacket later. I'm cold."

Oh, to be in the jacket's proximity and yet denied its snuggly embrace!

"Look what I found." Katie opens the cardboard box, revealing three black notebook computers. None of them work. I manage to stare into the box while continuing to leer at the jacket. Katie screams, "Take the damn box, I'm pregnant."

I hold the laptops like an archaeologist might hold the tooth of a dinosaur. "Where are they from?"

"I stole them. I can't believe you guys decided to do this here."

"We figured you'd be too pregnant to go anywhere else."

Dean rushes up behind me, sticks his red wire-brush beard into the box, and snatches forth a clunky old Thinkpad. He raises it to the sky. He taps the head of his pickaxe against the concrete, and a crowd gathers 'round.

We grant Adam the ceremonial first toss. Dean at bat. He swings the pickax just like Mickey Mantle, and the laptop splits into two pieces—screen-side and keyboard-side—before it ever hits the ground.

How broken can a thing get? When you can obliterate a computer without applying more than the slightest amount of force, what else is left to break?

But this thing was broken long before tonight.

We survey the initial bifurcation. Is it broken enough? No. It can break so much more. In this state—long before this state—the machine will no longer function. From here every subsequent descending level of destruction only describes how much difficulty will be involved in putting it all back together. Like Dante's levels of Hell: before you even reach Hell you are dead; the body no longer functions, but down and down you still must go. The user says the machine is broken. The user does not care how broken it is, he just wants it fixed. But the technician knows. It's his trade. The priest knows how desecrated a body can possibly become, and how difficult this will make his job in preparing the spirit for death.

Dean hands the axe over to Adam. We find joy in crushing the computers, every one of us connected to modernity's threat of the "rising machine"—the fear of domination by our own creation. But man made the pickaxe as well.

At one point a great blow tears the CD-ROM drive from the chassis, and a Microsoft Windows disk ejects like a driver through the windshield.

Silence descends for one brief moment. We all gather 'round. The disk is already broken. A piece of it has snapped off. The disk is useless. *Smash it*, we say. *Break it*, we say.

We pass the axe around. Some, drunk to the point of emotional assimilation with the tool, must be forcibly separated from it to give others a turn.

"The candy! Be careful of the candy!" Dean shrieks. He runs around, fingers aflame in his blaze of hair, and it becomes the mantra of the evening: "Don't break the candy."

The digital piñata exposes only further levels of itself, deeper layers of brokenness. Capacitors, circuit boards, transistor chips, plastic fan blades, wires, latches, screws. Strips of plastic and rubber: items no one expected to see launching out of such polite and sterile machines. Copper sheets crumple and writhe. Who would have expected so many moving parts? Peripherals, magnets, polished silver disks—no one can figure out what these are for. Cylinders. Objects of beauty and symmetry; tiny works of art hiding within. Bits that do nothing but direct the flow of energy.

But there's still so much more to break.

The CPU pops out. Smash it. There is nothing recognizable inside. Like the human brain, it is globular and homogeneous. In sharp contrast with the viscera. The viscera make sense like plumbing makes sense. Messy as it is, you can point out, *Yes here, this fits here and digestible matter flows from here to here where it sits. This place is where nutrients are extracted. Yes...* But the brain? Nothing but pulp. No place to say: *Thoughts flow from here to here and are analyzed here.* Nothing like that. And the processor chip is nothing like that either.

The chip is senseless, gutless, black-gray matter.

We're onto the third laptop and it feels like we've been swinging for ages. Going after little pieces like storks after crickets. Missing more than striking now, blasting chips from the street. Can it be broken even further? Transistors are severed. The keyboard keys, little helmets popping off the pogo hammers who close local circuits. Between these are layers of rubber and thin plastic. The screen itself reveals multiple levels of translucence. One clear slip comes loose, gets picked up, held up to a streetlight. The image fades to infrared on one side, ultraviolet on the other.

Our tone is a juggler's patch: menacing, vindictive, and playful. Striking with laughter. Be careful of the candy! Down with the fucking machines. "You ate my homework," someone cries, cursing the hard drive.

The batteries were removed before the smashing began. For safety perhaps, or for ceremony— symbolizing the swift, clean death offered by civilized society. Machines have their batteries removed all the time. Go to sleep. Go to sleep. Anesthetized, the laptop has no clue how many levels of brokenness it descends.

There is silence. The pickaxe falls to the ground. Dean scans the parking lot with wobbly eyes on his wobbly head. I notice Adam out there digging among the shrapnel, occasionally holding some broken part up to the light, looking for God-knows-what. Three laptops in tatters, eviscerated along the gravel. Thousands of pieces, bits and scrap from one corner of the old lot to the other—cracked, smashed, mangled.

"I'll put it all back together in the morning," slurs Dean, raising his bottle. "I'll glue it and duct tape it together. Save all the pieces. Don't lose any of the pieces! It'll be a work of art. A goddamn sculpture. I'll take some glue and fit it all in place and pretend it works. Think of how it'll look. The fucking screen is split in two! I'll slap some duct tape across the middle. I'll wrap it in string. I'll carry it to class and pretend to take notes. I'll bring it to a systems technician and tell them it just stopped working—see if they'll diagnose. I'll do this with a straight face. I don't know what's the problem, I'll say. I'm no good with these things, I'll say. I'll send it back on warranty. It just died, I'll say. I don't know what happened. It was fine the other day and then it just stopped working."

6.

By the third beer run, an utter failure due to standard alcohol laws which apparently no one at the party remembered, those of us not homeward bound or passed out on some coffin-sized segment of the floor no longer concern ourselves with clocks, causality, or coherence. The conversations crawl one over another like a colony of ants. All that remains is the tip of the tongue, the unleashing of everything unspoken during daylight hours.

"I don't enjoy oral sex—giving or receiving. I find it demeaning and impersonal."

"Well it's no handshake."

"I'm serious."

"Lacks the subtlety of a high five."

Tears and hugs accompany reckless kisses, tangled theories, rotten jokes. The conversations weave in and out and the word flows sloshing and sluggish from the resplendent lips of youth.

"We're leaving for tomorrow in two days!"

And…

"I want to be the guy who—you know, the guy in a little Japanese village with the old man who fights spiders."

And…

"I want to be the guy who tells the same old story over and over."

"Mila used to own a rat. She'd bring it into bars because it loved to drink."

"I love strawberries after sex. It's like rewarding yourself for having a good time."

"What would you do if you won a million dollars? I tell you what I'd do. I'd hire two private detectives to follow each other around."

"I want to be the guy who tells stories about flying badgers."

Someone says, "Did you see the party goat? That goat gets puked on more than any other goat in this history of goats."

I hear the question, "Aren't you an organ donor?"

And then the reply, "No, I still have to get it changed on my license."

And then, "You know it just means they won't try as

hard to save you."

Among the chatter, Will arrives. He and Dean and I sit down to pour overflowing shots and discuss the secrets of the universe. During the lulls in conversation, we stare into the fire's pulsing portals to red dimensions. Tiny glowing civilizations of coal. A log splits, crashing down in two pieces, crushing our visions. Dean and I gasp. We must have looks of complete devastation on our faces because Will flails his arms in mock panic and says, "Oh no! Our burning structure has collapsed into a burning structure. There's flames and debris everywhere, just like before," which puts things into perspective, and makes me wonder why among of all the zillions of chemical combinations in all the billions of galaxies out there, humans became so antagonistic toward disorder.

Dean seems to emerge from a coma. He slurs his words. "We're all just carved-out canyons of DNA. The same great ocean flows through us from one to the next to the next to the next…"

An unbroken chain of desire's flame and its extinguishing satisfaction.

The frenzy of generations, the distributed orgy of time—throwing ourselves against this mill of longing, ground by Kali's teeth into food for our own children. Sex-slaves performing at the whim of future generations, lured on by our descendants. Possessed to passion by spirits aching to exist. Here and now procreation resembles a mash of conflict, a dizzying delightful head-on collision of confusion, but I have seen the schematics of our unborn great great grandchildren. How they tug on our strings. Tributaries from distant futures, spawning upstream as time flows back toward our ancestors.

When our words fray hopelessly past the point of comprehension, Dean conducts one last toast. "To the little baby Katie and her little baby baby!"

7.

Dean and I drag each other up, and stumble into the living room. There we find Katie Ludwick in perfect posture on the couch, snug in our Jacket. Her lips part without a sound. Her eyes wide and horrified. Adam kneels beside her, yammering like a radiator with a loose gasket. He holds aloft a small silver disk, flat and metallic, a hole in the center like a washer. Probably some gizmo that flew out of one of the laptops. More than one witness to the event insists it's supposed to be like a wedding ring. Others posit that this is precisely what Adam wants us to think. Either way, there's no stopping him until the pressure drops. His torrent of words crash against the sides of his mouth, ricocheting off his lips like he's been carrying them around in there all these months. As if he composed each word the night she kicked him out and has just been waiting for the right moment to release them. They are the words of a man on his deathbed uncorking his soul. I don't know if it's the alcohol or the alignment of the stars, but his voice bears neither desperation nor doubt. He says what he says because it needs to be said, not because he thinks it will make a damn bit of difference. I only wish I'd heard it from the beginning.

8.

"… and in my imagination I erase all the stupid things I've ever told you, and we get to start over again for the first time. I pretend we meet at a party like this one. I come around the corner and there you are. Our eyes lock long enough to get past whatever it is that keeps people from really connecting with each other. You know, that specific amount of time where the brain panics and people get nervous and look away. But we stare too long and too deep for strangers, too long even for friends. Standing there shaking hands and not letting go. I say, I'm Adam, and you say, I'm Katie. Hi, I say. Hi, you say—all this with our eyes like a hall of mirrors, thoughts bouncing between us faster than pheromones. Oh Katie—see? You're looking at me like that now. This is what I'm talking about. This is a reason for us to need each other. And so, okay, in my imagination we both try to get back in, to regain eye contact, to see if we can beat the record. But... but here's the problem, see... You and I, we're competition. A threat to the failed love affairs of history, and they're all conspiring to keep us apart... The universe always fighting back, but we beat the odds. When I leave the party, you find a way to become my ride home. We end up back at my apartment. It doesn't matter that you don't have a car. It doesn't matter that I don't have an apartment. I've pre-imagined the apartment I would have, all down to the last detail. I invite you in and all we do is talk, but not a lot. Not as much as I usually talk. You talk more than I do, because—you know—because I'm nervous and I love the sound of your voice. You're making your way from room to room, getting a drink, clearing off the table, kneeling beside me to show off your latest zine or some art from your backpack. Look—you say—I cut up this old shirt and made a dress out of it. That's one thing you say, and I think it's pretty great. I keep trying to catch your eye again, but neither of us push it. We sit on the floor beside the couch, and you tell me about your mother. You tell me about the first Madonna cassette you bought, and a little story about something that happened in high school. It's a good story and I laugh and spend a few minutes thinking about it. You ask me if I'd like to hold hands, maybe just for a minute, just to see how it feels. How does it feel? I imagine how it feels—I remember how it feels. Our fingers interlock and fit. All fingers interlock and fit, though, right? That's the universe trying to stop us. Okay, yeah, but not like this, I think. Look at these hands, Katie. Do you remember? You ask, *Do you want to kiss me?* and I say, *Can I?* And... you find my reply kind of weird so you don't respond—but then I kiss you anyway, holding your face with one hand. We are warm and thundering. And it's like... it's like... it's like lightning splitting a tree and the sparks set the forest floor on fire. Oh God, we didn't expect that. But we ride it out... we ride it out... It's like we're trying to find that precise amount of eye contact where there's no going back. We feel each other out, but you won't lose control. There are so many reasons not to lose control. Not for someone like me, not for someone who doesn't have an apartment or a job or a future. Not for someone so strange and so reckless. You know you have to be careful choosing a mate. You can stop this, you think, but then you imagine me in tears, heartbroken. You feel like all hearts are fated to break, and you're worried you'll break mine and that I'll feel it all the way down because I love you so much, and... maybe I won't ever stop breaking. You worry maybe I'll just keep trying to make it work, to get you back, to overtake you—but you won't submit. You can't submit. The universe has eyes everywhere. Now I'm outside your window and you can hear me saying: *Don't go. Don't go. I need you.* Or... I want to need you. Am I supposed to need you or not? I mean, am I supposed to be aloof or adoring or what? I'm just who I am, Katie, and I know none of these words make sense to you, either in my imagination or in reality, but this is where I fit. You are where I belong. However I try to imagine it, however the scenario goes down in my head, I'm always under your window begging for you to take me back. I'm staring at our twin telephones wherever I go, sitting on every wall and countertop and coffee table I see. You are more beautiful than all the first winter nights. You're like those little crystal snowlets when it hasn't even snowed yet—that just hang in the air and dangle on spider webs. You're the kind of sunset that causes shipwrecks. You're a crystal ocean washing up to the shores of a red desert or something where the moon is bigger than the sun and lions stalk on mesas of vineyards of gypsum, or... and... what am I even talking about? But listen. And... and Katie, when I'm old and in a rocking chair, and I look over, I'm going to see your face, whether you're there with me or not."

CHAPTER FIVE

RIVER

Missoula, MT

AND THEN THERE WAS the time I rescued the girl from the pit.

Public works had dug a massive hole out of a street corner somewhere in the U district. They were trying to get to a pipe problem, but it was going to take longer than they originally thought, so they blocked it off with sawhorses, police tape, plastic orange fencing, and nasty notes. The pit sat there all weekend just waiting for lovely ladies to climb down inside.

She was half-Japanese and all kinds of adorable. I was on a walk and had only glanced over the warning signs and into the hole because it's the sort of thing I can't resist. I expected nothing but dirt and pipes and the unearthed guts and tendons of urban reality. Instead, I found a pair of eyes shaded by ten-foot lashes.

"Hello there," I said.

"Hi."

"What are you doing?"

"Oh you know, just sitting around. In this pit."

She was beautiful. Normally I don't tell women they are beautiful when I first meet them, because they have a tendency to run away. But this one wasn't going anywhere.

"You're beautiful," I said.

"Thanks," she said. "I bet you say that to all the girls you find trapped in pits."

Turns out she was just curious about how cold the dirt was at that depth and she had to find out. She'd crawled down just fine, but much like the proverbial cat in the tree, discovered it was not as easy to get back up. And dressed all in white, too. I figured she must care a lot about strata temperatures.

"How long have you been down there?"

"About an hour," she said.

"And no one's found you?"

"No one looks in holes anymore. You and I are a dying breed."

I tried to find something she could grab onto. There isn't a lot lying around in residential neighborhoods useful for rescuing girls from pits. I could have climbed down in there with her, but then we'd both be trapped.

She told me the dirt was crumbly and cold. Then I remembered how peasant revolts are sometimes waged with farm tools. When necessary, hammers and sickles will double as weapons. Every house on every block has a tool shed or a garage.

"Listen," I said. "I'm not trying to get into a philosophical discussion while you're stuck down there, but isn't it interesting? If Missoula was ever invaded, all these people could rise up with their shovels and lawn mowers and chain saws."

"Sure, but everyone in Montana has a gun anyway," she said.

"Good point."

"You know, this would be an awesome conversation to have around, say, coffee... somewhere on, say, top of the street."

I told her I'd be right back and ran down the block, looking for a rake or something. The yards here were tidy. Not a tool left over; everything locked up in the sheds.

But on the next block I found what I needed. Someone had left a garden hose out. Now all I had to do was a bit of breaking and entering. I considered knocking to ask permission, but then whoever answered would want to get involved with the rescue, and I didn't want to share the glory. I crept over to the spigot and released the hose, then dragged it out to the street.

Back at the pit, I had a thought.

"I don't mean to be a dick," I said. "But what sort of effect is this rescue going to have?"

"About nine or ten feet of elevation," she said.

"I mean emotionally. If I help you out, is it going to reflect a lack of backbone? I mean, if I'm just running around doing things for you like a servant boy. You may not respect me afterward."

"I see your point."

"And I wouldn't want there to be any sense of obligation, either. Like for you to feel as if you have to repay me somehow."

"It's complicated."

"I just don't want to put that kind of pressure on you."

"How sweet," she said. "I suppose I should just find my own way out."

"What if I just held the hose and you climb up on your own," I suggested. "I won't pull or anything."

"No heroics?"

"Promise."

It was more than enough for the job. She only needed that little extra. I let her do most of the work, and with a few mountaineering steps she was on the street.

"Great rescue," she said, gazing up at me through the euphoria of newfound freedom.

"How does it feel?" I asked. "Obligation-wise and respect-wise."

She teetered on her heels. "You know, I had this weird thought while you were finding the hose. I was imagining the moment I climb over the edge and get out, how you'd look into my eyes and see a certain sparkle there. And I'd see a certain sparkle in yours too. And then those sparkles would cross paths and meet in the middle, between our faces, and like, high five or something, creating a big booming sparkly hypnotic moment fluttering around our heads."

"But that didn't happen?"

"Not really."

She ran her fingers through her hair and spun a full circle on her toes, all the while looking at the clouds. Then she walked toward me. Her hands groped the air a few inches from my chest.

"Boy, there's something about being rescued from a pit, though. Triggers the reptile brain."

"Maybe you should go with that," I said.

"I don't know," she said, "I think I'm a little too grateful. Like you were saying. It's risky to base relationships on obligatlon."

"Relationships?"

"I'm just not comfortable feeling beholden. You wouldn't respect me for it later. How about this," she said. "It's a small world. Let's go our separate ways, and when fate brings us together, the time will be right."

That sounded reasonable and exciting. She hugged me and scurried off into the wooded rural wilderness.

I never saw her again.

1.

I wake up on top of the washer and dryer. A trail of bodies leads from the basement into Katie's apartment, where they've conscripted as pillows anything mildly lumpy—stuffed animals, balled-up sweaters, a towel wrapped around a dictionary. They share couches, chairs, and beanbags. They squeeze onto the great oval rug in the center of the floor like castaways on a raft, huddled under the piles of blankets Katie keeps on reserve.

I go to pee and find Adam snoring away in the bathtub.

Only Katie is awake. Sitting on the front porch reading the Independent and drinking coffee.

"Hey," I say, rubbing my face.

"Baby's first bender," she says.

"They're all dead in there. You killed them."

"I know, they were annoying."

"What are we going to do with the bodies?"

"Fuck it."

Back inside, I think about making breakfast. I count seventeen passed-out patrons, but I'm sure there must be more curled up in strange nooks. Too much work, I decide, and put on another pot of coffee instead.

One by one they come back to life in various states of consciousness, bearing reluctant good mornings and woeful proclamations of hangovers and shuffling steps. Katie fires up a pan of hash browns.

"Why do we have to worry about food every single day?" I ask. "Wouldn't it be more efficient if everyone just spent all Saturday gorging ourselves to store up for the rest of the week?"

"I love eating," Katie says.

Someone I don't recognize walks by.

"Killer party."

"What happened to the goat?"

No one mentions Adam's declaration of love. We all do a pretty good job pretending it never happened. When he emerges from the bathroom, he's got devastation and terror all over his face. He talks to us about his dreams and keeps glancing at Katie like he expects her to come over and club him in the head with one of her cast-iron pans.

After a few minutes, she brings Adam a cup of coffee. She stands beside him as he takes a sip. "Too hot?" she says. "A little," he says. "Need any sugar or anything?" she says. "It's perfect," he says.

She doesn't walk away. Seems to stare at his elbow. He keeps on sipping and does not stop sipping because the minute he takes a break from the coffee he knows he will have to acknowledge the fact that she is standing there, and then he will have to look at her or maybe say something. When the cup is dry, he keeps pretending to drink until all the attention in the room has wandered away from him. Only then does he whisper, "That was good coffee," as Katie leads him into the kitchen by the empty cup. There they talk in low, serious voices, but I can't make out a word.

2.

In the days that follow, Adam drops by the house from time to time. His visits are always brief. Five or ten minutes tops. Most of the time he engages us as a group, then takes Katie aside for a few private words before leaving. Amelia antagonizes him, demanding to know why Katie should even consider taking him back.

I spend too much of my time chasing the jacket.

On the night of the party Katie had put it in her closet, and Dean, drunk out of his mind, grabbed it and used it for a pillow. He took it home with him when he left. I could have screamed, but I let it go. Give it time. All jackets come to those who wait. But when I finally went over to his place, Katie had already recovered it.

The jacket bounced around this way as if by divine intervention. Even Adam ended up wearing it around for a day, which was the last time I saw it. But he seemed so anxious about Katie that I couldn't bear to take it away from him. I asked him for it later and he told me he left it at Dean's. Maybe it's time to give up and let the jacket chase me for a change.

Katie Ludwick starts spending a lot more time sleeping. Her doctor says she's only weeks away. Her belly keeps growing. Soon she'll fill the whole apartment.

3.

Two Sunday morning's after the party, Katie Ludwick wakes me up with a tap on the head and says, "Let's go fishing."

I tell her she's too pregnant to fish. She tells me to shut the hell up. She holds her rod and hands me her fishing vest. Says she has her dad's car for the weekend and is going to use it. She hasn't had a chance to fish all summer and by the time the baby's born and she goes through all the postpartum blah blah blah and settles down to the reality of this living creature, at least to the point where she'll maybe be willing to leave it in her mother's care for more than five minutes, the rivers will be too low and fishing will be for shit.

"Is leaving town really such a good idea?" I say.

"It's the best idea," she says. "It's the only idea."

And what if she suddenly goes into labor?

"Then my kid will be born in the woods and I won't have to register her into society. She'll be a non-existent baby, just like her non-existent daddy."

"Okay, but it isn't safe. What would the doctor say?"

"She'd tell me to stop asking stupid questions," Katie says. "You go get my brother. I'll pick up Amelia. Meet us at Butterfly and we'll leave from there."

"I was going to go to the library," I say.

"Don't you know it's against the law in Montana for single women to go fishing alone?"

"Fine," I say. And that settles it.

Las Vegas, NV

The weeks between the morning when she left me for good and the day I caught that Greyhound back to Missoula will always remain a blur, hard enough to piece together in my mind, even harder to put into words. But the last time I saw her face remains as clear and present to me now as my own surroundings.

I followed her out of her apartment. I carried her accordion for her. She kept saying things from the doorway. "You were meant to be a spark in a million eyes, not a furnace in one," and "I need something stable," and "Someone I can rely on."

I ignored it all. My mind wouldn't stop looping the endless mantra: *This is it.*

A singular moment with no context, as adrift as raw existence. *This is it.* Staring at her ass without lust or emotion, as she dragged the small suitcase down the stairs, toy wheels thumping with each step. *This is it.* The zipper on the side-pouch half open, and nothing I could have done to stop her.

I am familiar with so many systems of decay, so many structures that break down, step-by-step, through natural processes. But the loss of love feels like a cruel joke under hypnosis. Sometimes things just go away.

My last memory of her is posed like a boutique display on the other side of a passenger seat window. She got in his truck and closed the door. The truck rolled forward, its window frame dragging her into the desert and out of my life. Gone for good and for always. Only imprints remained in my mind. I'll never forget that last look we exchanged through the semi-tinted glass, blending us beyond any touch—her snug in a seat belt, me standing outside in the Vegas swelter, sweating, unable to move.

I remember noticing my reflection in the window superimposed over her real face on the other side—closer than we'd ever been in life, close enough for each to be the other. Then one last look of horror as she let herself realize this was it. Her eyes in my head, my lips on her chin, our hair tangled flat and colorless in the glass.

It. That's what this was.

She left with her eyes in my head, and I saw

everything the way she must have been seeing it for weeks.

My lips on her chin. Her eyes on my forehead. Was she trying to swap reflections and leave herself one last thing to come back for? Like all the little bits and ribbons left in my pockets over the preceding weeks, the buttons and receipts in my backpack.

We were a tangle long before that window got between us.

The first time I realized it was after a hot shower. She'd got out to dry her hair, leaving me standing there with the last of the water drizzling down my back. I looked down and saw her toes growing out of my knees. I jumped out to show her, but by then they were back on her feet. Later that night I kissed her shoulder and when I pulled back my lips stayed behind. My fingers got snared in her hair and detached. She left an ear on my chest one morning like a pillow mint. Before long, I found myself reaching for things I didn't even like. A jar of green olives in the fridge, a can of baby corns. Only her fingers had ever reached for these things before. One day she whistled while reading a book, but she'd always said she never learned how. I caught myself twirling my hair… or was it her hair? We started pointing out the sorts of things only the other had ever noticed before.

That day in the window, when our faces mingled in their reflections, there was a moment where she seemed to wear my lips. She was telling me with my own lips how complete the end this was about to be in five short seconds... four... three... leaving her eyes in my head... two... one... the gunning engine... zero. Some secret desire or fear or boredom had driven her to that moment, and then she was gone. The truck rolled on, leaving me alone in a cloud of dust.

To this day, I don't know what she took with her and what she left behind. My thumbs seem smaller. I'm pretty sure.

4.

Dean lives about a mile east of Katie. His small ground-floor apartment looks vacant from the outside, with its long empty porch and dark windows. I drum my fingers on the door, but there's no reply. I knock louder. Still nothing. I try the handle, but it's locked. I run around to the side-door. Also locked. Rest my ear up against the glass, I hear voices inside. The beep of an answering machine. The voices continue.

Returning to the front porch, I find his door ajar. I can see a brass chain measuring the dark gap.

"It's me," I say.

The door closes, the chain comes down, and Dean lets me in. Beeeeeep goes the machine.

"Why are your lights off?" I ask.

Dean shushes me, slumps down on his couch. He grabs his box of messages from the coffee table, drops it in his lap, and presses play. I recognize the voice of his ex-wife. He rewinds and we listen again:

"Don't get me wrong, Dean, please don't. You have to understand if it were in any way possible for me to have avoided this call, to have not had to track down your number—a process that, by the way, took eleven days and required going out for 'drinks' with Max Kessler—I would have. My God, Dean, and it's not that I didn't want to talk to you, but I have come to fully comprehend your revulsion at the very idea of me, much less the possibility of having to share the same airspace and endure what may be an endless stream of thoughts, emotions, and confessions. But—and when I say but, please keep in mind that I am not trying in any way to be contrary or to start a veritable war of words—but I have had no choice. I've wanted to call you for months now, even longed for it now and then, yet I have this entire time had what I felt was a choice. And that choice was grounded upon what I considered to be a well-developed respect for your feelings. Yes, Dean, your feelings, believe it or not, are a presence to me, and like a seed that a gardener plants and leaves to the elements—out of sight out of mind they say—but which germinates and sprouts and can no longer be ignored, a full appreciation for your emotional investment has at last come to light, and despite my own compulsions, and even *need* from time to time to visit you and impose upon you whatever ferocious manifestations of ovulation might have on any particular day reared its proverbial ugly head, I did not. I refused. I put your feelings first. Something I never perhaps did while we were (as it were) 'together' has become the absolute foundation for determining my own actions in this situation. And Dean, the situation has changed.

"Please don't erase this message until you've heard me out. There are things… important things… all I need right now is to know you have been in earshot while I say these things. Dean, I know you won't believe me, but I really was in love with you. Truly, I was. I didn't even know it then maybe, but I've come to realize, which just makes everything I did to you even worse. The point is—God, what is the point? Alright, here's the point… No. It's no use to tell you any of this, not even for my own benefit. I had some vague romantic notion of purging, of pushing out the gunk and the shit, but really there's too much. There's the me with the guilt, and there's the me who wants you to fall in love with me again so I can laugh in your face and call you a little boy and walk out, and there's the me who wants you to fall in love with me again so that I can kiss your sweet lips, swallow my own poison and die. There's the practical me, there's the slap in the face, there's the angry, there's the possessed, there's the giddy and the girly. I've got—no, look, I'm trying to speak clearly. I should have just sent you a letter. And to think I'm running away again. I am, you know. I'm moving very far away and you'll never see me. And the thing is, Dean, I have a child. And she's yours. You're thinking how could I possibly know that, and you're right, but I do. And it kills me that you'll never know her. But I can trace it all back, and it all makes sense. I even knew at the time. I did. I could feel it taking hold. I could feel your silly spirit rushing into me. But I took everything from you, didn't I? I took everything and you're just a shell now and I'm moving away and I can't care what happens to you. I can't, but I do, but not enough to do anything about it. I don't know why I even called, really, but you had to know, I suppose. And now it's done, I've said exactly nothing I planned on saying, so... bye."

5.

Dean goes to play it a third time. I ask him how long he's been sitting here listening to that message. Since yesterday, he says.

His face is a blank wall, and I can't think of any good way to respond to that, so I tell him we're going fishing.

"Sounds fun," he says.

"No, see, you have to come with us."

"I can't," he says.

"Why not?"

"I can't leave."

"Why not?"

"I can't ever leave," he says.

"Ever?"

"I have everything I need. I've been preparing for this moment."

I check out his kitchen. The fridge is full of gallon-jugs of water and ketchup bottles. Bags of frozen blueberries in the freezer. His cupboards packed full of non- and semi-perishables: cans of fruit, beans, bags of rice, wheat-free noodles, tomato sauce. There's soup, soup, and more soup. Chocolate bars in all the drawers.

"You can't stay here forever," I say. "Your sister wants you to go fishing with her."

"I'm a dad."

"So it appears. Then again, that woman is crazy."

"Yeah."

"Let's go."

"We'll never make it across town."

"Your sister is going to have a baby soon. You want to be there for that, right?"

"The child is an implant," he says. "All of them are. A rising generation born to bury us."

Dean presses play. I grab the answering machine and make it stop. He whimpers a little but does not protest. "Seriously, how long have you been torturing yourself with this?"

"Only a few days."

"She's fucking with you, Dean. She knows what buttons to push. I doubt any of it's true."

"It's all true," he says. "Everything is true. I'm under surveillance. They're using her to scare me into the open."

I recall the time Dean daydreamed Romanian spies into old Coupe de Villes and pointed out eighty-year-old ladies with cameras in their eyelids.

"That's stupid," I say.

He looks at me with horrified wide eyes that narrow slowly with suspicion like pupils contracting in the light.

"Jacket," I say. "Where's your jacket?"

As of this morning, I'd almost come to terms with the possibility of never seeing it again, much less wearing it—but now the need is desperate. This is the moment, goddammit. I run around the apartment, looking everywhere.

"On the microwave," he tells me.

I return to him, holding it in my hands. I can feel its cuddliness nuzzling my fingertips. I hold it up to Dean's face.

"See this? Do you know why I've wanted this so badly? It keeps you invisible from classified technology."

Dean gives me that look. Crazy people aren't stupid, and they know when you're patronizing them.

"Fine," I relent. "But it'll still keep you warm. Come on, you don't have a choice. The pregnant lady demands it."

I can see the gears whirring in his head—his brain trying to reconcile and integrate his sister's desires with his current picture of reality. Whatever finally makes it all click is buried so far inside Dean's mind I probably wouldn't have understood even if he'd explained it to me.

"Yes," he says. "We have to go. But we have to go the secret way."

"Okay," I say, helping him into the jacket. "Secret way it is."

"Zozezaz," he whispers.

6.

Outside, the sun is busy swatting clouds out of its face. I let Dean lead the way, and we follow the sound of the river.

He crouches low, walking faster than usual. Every now and then he stops and looks back to make sure I'm still there. I'm jealous he gets to wear that jacket. It's just so damn comfy. We cross Orange Street, head north, and creep into the park where we take shelter under the bridge. Shelter from what, I wonder?

"The sky is a seamless dome of hexagonal mirrors," Dean says.

I look up and see faces, vegetables, dragons. Some see moisture vapor. Others see heaven.

"Katie's waiting for us at Butterfly," I say.

"We'll have to call her. Butterfly is not an option. And we can't cross the bridge. Too many passenger cars. Our only way over the river is by the tracks."

There's an unused railroad bridge spanning the Clark Fork River between Broadway and a no-man's-land filled with slouching fences and abandoned building. About a half-mile away in the opposite direction, but Dean's the boss. He leads me under the bridge and over a fence that explicitly tells us what pieces of shit citizens we are for crossing it. We creep through an abandoned mid-century horse stable I like to call *the airplane hangar*. We huddle in the dark and wait for invisible helicopters to fly by. Dean checks the perimeter. He picks up a rock and throws it out into the field, waiting to see what happens. Nothing happens.

Then we cross the tracks. These things have been out of commission for years. Dean watches the sky. He insists we touch no rail or any other form of metal in case they're monitoring the area via low-voltage conductive flow. So we hop from wooden plank to wooden plank. The grandfatherly old Clark Fork tumbles below like a prairie of tiny turbines.

What he's going through today is a retreat into the safe places of his mind. They may not seem safe with all the hexagonal mirrors and spy cameras and government agents and Hopi witch doctors on his trail, but trust me—it's infinitely safer than the parts of his mind where his ex-wife still hangs out. Paranoia takes

Dean back to a more innocent world—of television shows and marijuana, playing spies with the neighborhood kids, freaking each other out in the dark. A world of predetermined tensions and resolutions. Some familiar territory, navigable only via coded pathways and personal incantations.

Once across, we don't turn toward town but keep north, hopping over to a perpendicular set of tracks. We push past the knapweed fields and trickle into the lovable Northside, a neighborhood I most fondly remember for ogling over crystals of MSG as if it was a controlled substance. This section of town doubles as a museum for Old Industry—last century's booms: the rail and wheel, the oil-hemorrhaging champions of transportation. Arrhythmic aberrations of night, and the things that truly go bump therein, echo with deep bovine groans of machinery—the shudder and clash of train cars, an occasional blast of steam, an eighteen-wheeler coming or going.

Dean grins for the first time. We press our backs against a giant rusting oil drum. A pay phone clings to the wall of a gas station, way over on the far side of a gravel lot littered like with land mines of crushed beer cans.

"I'm going to go for it," I say.

"Okay," Dean says.

"Unless you'd rather."

"I'll keep a lookout here."

I walk over to the phone booth. Baffled, I hold up the

receiver. I need thirty-five cents now? Since when? I find the number for Butterfly Herbs and ask to speak with Katie.

"What's taking you so long?"

"This is weird," I say, staring at the silver lock on the phone's box body. "Who comes and empties out all the quarters?"

"We need to get on the road."

"Dean's having a bad day," I explain.

"Well hurry up. The sun's getting high."

Per Dean's instructions, I tell Katie to pick us up by the Interstate. I tell her we're going to pretend to be hitchhikers, and Dean wants her to pull over as if we don't know each other but just randomly decided to pick us up. Then we will get in the car. She laughs and hangs up the phone.

We wait near the on-ramp. He casts silent spells on cars as they pass us by. Some hippies in a van stop and ask if we need a ride. Dean tells them we already have one and sticks out his thumb.

Ten minutes later, a white '77 Cadillac with one working brake light scrapes off into the gravel shoulder a couple dozen yards ahead of us. Amelia opens the passenger door and we crawl into the back seat. Adam is there, rolling cigarettes.

"Hey guys, how are you?"

He asks this in such a genuine fashion—I don't think small talk is even a concept he's aware of.

For some reason, neither Dean nor myself are

capable of answering his question. At last Katie says, "They're fine."

My Ridiculous Childhood

I haven't yet mentioned my ridiculous childhood. I fell in love for the first time at age seven. Ha ha, you laugh. How cute. Puppy love. No. This was the real thing. Dead serious. From the age of seven, I chased this girl for two years with unwavering determination. I might be chasing her to this day had my parents not decided to move to Montana. I wrote epitomes of love, saved up for jewelry, even sang a'cappella in an assembly room of parents and students, dedicating the song to her. A younger initiate into the dour secrets of the heart there may never have been.

Her name was Rachael. She was golden-haired and at least four inches taller than me. She refused my elaborate romance, and returned nothing more than friendship. Later, once I'd resigned myself to a life without her affections, I turned away from her type and have pursued darker-haired, shorter ladies ever since. Not a single blonde has touched these lips. It took me about twenty-eight months to give up my pre-pubescent pursuit of Rachael. Oh, how I pined. How many thousands of tears I wept. The vows I made to myself and to God, at a mere nine years old, swearing on my life never to love again, that if I could not have her, then I would be the last of my bloodline—neither marriage nor children. So far it's stuck.

I wonder if I've damned myself to the chase. I try to trace back my restless tendencies, my surges of romance and subsequent withdraw from intimacy, my inability to stay in one place for longer than a few months. Could it all come down to unrequited love at a tender age when most boys still think girls are infested with the plague? If Missoula rescued me from my earliest passion, maybe that's why I continue to use her this way: as a place of safe return, entrusting her to resolve all conflicts.

Occasionally, I still get a glimpse of that seven-year-old me hiding way down in my brain, pulling the homuncular levers. Childhood is a secret whispered into the ear that we spend the rest of our lives trying to remember.

7.

Katie Ludwick turns off at Bonner and follows Highway 200 toward a new fishing spot she wants to try. Amelia's feet burden the dash. We all stare at the windows. The woods are bright and still. Afternoon is coming on, bugs are off to nap, and Katie grumbles about what a horrible time it is to go fishing.

Taking a narrow trail through the bushes, we reach the river where a small embankment displays bleach white stones. Nearby, the tide has, over the years, slapped a little shelf into the dirt. Amelia and I sit in the shade among an intricate system of tree roots. Dean stares through dangling leaves. Adam rolls cigarettes for Amelia and holds court with everyone—a question here, a story there, and gestures of affirmation for all.

The river is calm and shallow for several feet, until a deep vein bubbles up a cascade of ripples. Katie will fish just within those ripples. She puts on her waders, assembles her pole, and ties a fat fly to the end of her line. Downstream, a row of four naked pylons span one bank to the other. The bridge has been gone for years, but her legs remain. Steel rods and rims of rubble fray forth from the concrete scalps of each crumbling monument.

"I thought fish didn't bite at noon," Adam says.

Katie tells him he doesn't know anything and to just shut up, and then she leans closer into his body. One hand holds his arm for balance and the other goops up her fly. Before she hits the river, she rests her fingertips on his cheek and kisses him. Her lips get lost in his beard, and I tell myself I knew this would happen even though part of me was scared it might not.

"Well," Amelia says. "Will you tell me about Vegas now?"

Adam and Dean are out of earshot, pointing out various plants and insects to one another. Katie lifts her rod to the sky. She sways on her ankles, rocking back and forth on the brittle shore. Her line catches in the breeze and she lets out a little extra. Stepping into the river, she lets out a little more. Leans to the right, tilts her pole. Her fly snaps to attention and her line tugs into the wind.

And then, because I have nothing better to do, I tell

Amelia everything. How Vegas Girl was dating some other guy from Iowa the entire time we were together. How I found out by running out of money and getting evicted, so that I showed up at her place with all my stuff while the guy from Iowa was staying over. Having nowhere else to go I spent the night on her couch. Iowa boy slept in her room. We'd been up until 3am trying to talk it out. A conversation dense with silence that sheltered our voices. She spoke in a light breeze, and I, a drop or two of rain. Communication going nowhere she slipped off to her room, leaving me with a pillow and a blanket. Even with the door closed I could hear them talking from down the hall. Their words meandered through the hollow of the house, reaching my ears like a foreign language. "Wellamso ab hilblim," she said. "Donfy leeba, yobofro lyd," was his reply. These phrases dwindled to moans and sighs, an arrhythmic creaking of bedsprings against the syncopated thud of wood on wall.

I tell Amelia how I survived the night by remembering Dean once lived with his ex-wife and her boyfriend for two months. The next morning I moved into a hostel near the Strip and started the slow bounce back to finding my balls again. But then she met me in a coffee shop and told me the whole story. Apparently she'd been in love with this Iowa guy since high school. I always thought ours was the epic romance, but I turned out to be the side dish. They'd been through years of struggling back and forth, him never making a commitment, always traveling around the country, visiting now and again to sweep her off her feet, then dashing off again. A fiery passion that never quite seemed to work out. Now he was off to North Carolina or something. She'd broken up with him for good this time, she said. She wanted to be with me now. There are two or three women in the world who I can say 'no' to only until they ask. For one more month we were happy. I think mostly she felt bad for me because I was homeless in Las Vegas, though I'm sure she must have loved me in some small way. But when the guy from Iowa had a change of heart and drove up again in his truck, she melted right under the door, dripped down the stairs, and seeped into his cab.

I tell Amelia how I ran after her. How I stood at the car window. Her hand on the glass. My face in her face. How the muffler coughed to life and took her away.

"Oh, dear," Amelia says. She takes my hand and we watch the river.

Dean and Adam hold a large piece of driftwood between them, the way two paramedics might hold a stretcher. They're just staring at each other. Adam's jaw is moving. Always moving. Rhythmic, fatherly, story after story. He'll make an amazing dad.

"Anyway," I say.

"Yeah," Amelia says. She puts her fingers in my hair, smoking with her other hand. "So what's next?"

I scratch my face and breathe all the air out of my

lungs. I don't intend to say anything more. But staring at the palms of my empty hands, I feel the words, "I'm afraid," come out. "Afraid that if I keep moving from place to place, I'll miss something important. Something you don't get to see unless you sit still for a long time. But what can I do? Whenever I try to stay put, I freak out about the rest of the world moving on without me. I can't make up my mind. I can't make up my mind about anything."

She grips the back of my neck and speaks in a low, soft voice.

"The road is your rebellion against growing old," she says. "From our point of view, you're the one standing still."

Dean climbs around on the rocks. The jacket looks good on him. I think maybe it really does keep him safe. He seems calmer out in nature, trading in his worries for a jacket and a piece of driftwood. I can relate. Everything I want is here. Everything except the sweet longing to return.

Amelia watches the soft pebbles of the riverbank. She reaches into her purse and hands me a silver disc of polished aluminum. It's the little ring of metal Adam found among the laptop guts the night of the party, which he held up in front of Katie while pouring out guts of his own. No pride or desperation. The ring feels like liquid between my fingers. I wonder what sort of system it belonged to. What it did. What it was for.

"You couldn't even fit a pinky through this," I laugh.

"Why do you have it?"

"They gave it to me in the car. He said he's going to get her a proper ring, but this one belongs to all of us. I think you should hold on to it for a while."

Then she wraps her silver-sleeves around my neck, hanging onto me in that sideways way that makes it impossible to hug back. We sit there for a long time until drained of unspoken words. Why do we do it? Why do we keep coming back to that place, prowling for each other, making the slow approach, teasing into kisses, when we know—when we *know* without any doubts, experientially we know, statistically we know— that it won't work out and will only end in pain and suffering. We keep stepping onto the painted X, slipping into the trap, opening our hearts, undressing every layer, saying the same words. And all the while echoes of the crash creep over our shoulders, whispering into our ears as I whisper into hers.

"Really, Joshua," she whispers back, "you always pick the strangest times to say these things."

8.

Katie is hip-deep now, blank-faced, well into the groove. Her casts harmonize with the river breeze. Water splashes up under her round and perfect belly.

Dean walks over and shows us a bug on a twig he's been carrying around. He adds, "All of us here right now, we are all cut from the same cloth."

Adam calls out to Katie, "How goes it?"

"Not one goddamn strike," she says.

We make sandwiches and spread them out on the smooth side of an old log. Dean keeps wandering off to speak to the bushes. Sometimes he refuses to open his eyes for minutes at a time because visual information is a construct imposed upon him, fabricated by forces attempting to lead him into a false sense of self. When I ask if I can wear the jacket for a while, he hugs it close to his chest.

Amelia stands up and lobs rocks into the river, trying to see if she can break it. Katie yells at her to stop. "You're scaring the fish!"

"That is my intention," Amelia says. "I am a savior of fish."

Dean cues off of this and flings riverward a stone of his own. He stares at the point where ripples heal over the splash. He raises his arms high, allowing them to sway. His fingers wiggle in the wind and the river massages the shore. Dean is not defined by a career or a family or politics or a home; he is defined only by the music in the movements of his arms, arms which now drift in time with his sister's gentle casts. The sleeves on his jacket flutter like the wings of a caddis fly.

Katie is yelling back to us that she's just about ready to take a break when something flashes on the river. None of us see it, but later we will all swear we did. Katie's line goes tight. Her wrists tense. Her rod becomes a question mark. Her leader a spotlight upon the surface of the waters.

"She's got one," Adam says.

"How big is it?" I ask.

"Feels pretty big," Katie says. She looks like a pregnant Norse goddess with her blond hair blazing in the sunlight, arms held high as if brandishing a spear or a bolt of lightning.

"Does she have a net?"

"Katie Ludwick needs no net!"

Dean stands on the stump of a tree and orchestrates the event, mimicking his sister's motions. His lips move: *Zozezaz*.

Katie's huge splashing steps toward shore alternate with moments of utter quiescence. Sometimes she reels in a few clicks, other times she gives it some slack. Whenever she reels, Dean's fingers flare and stab outward like bear claws; when she lets go, his head bows over in weariness. When she shouts, his lips move. *Zozezaz*. Katie never releases more than she reels in. She adjusts the tension on the line ever so slightly. The tip of her rod is epileptic.

"It's pretty big," she screams. "Get my net!"

"Katie Ludwick needs no net," Adam says.

"You didn't bring one," I say.

"Yes I did, it's in my bag."

"No it isn't."

"Goddammit, look again!"

I look again. Her bag is empty.

"Goddammit. Goddammit!"

We all start to laugh—well, Adam and I do—Dean continues engaging in his sympathetic magic as Amelia ignores us to pick flowers. If I had a net, I would gather them all up in one swoop, all these spirits I've known for years and their ceaselessly aging bodies. I'd place each of them in a town exactly like Missoula, in houses and apartments exactly like the ones they live in now, in relationships and problems and confusions no different from those they've been muddling through all their lives. I would put on Katie's jacket and leave them behind and follow the river to the mouth of the sea where my clothes would be drenched and brambles tear into my flesh and my lungs fill up with water—until I could figure out a way to come back home and find them all unchanged.

"Think it'll get away?" Adam says.

"Hell no," I say.

"Goddammit," Katie shouts. This time her cries are a curse over the waters. "Goddammmmmmmm!" The word catches in her throat and eases into a groan. For an instant the tip of her rod drops way too low, and she seems to stagger—but the moment passes and she falls right back into form. But her groan doesn't stop. It grows louder, rising in pitch to become a wail.

"Is she okay?"

"Are you okay?"

"I'm going to have a fucking baby," she screams.

"It took her nine months to figure this out?"

"I think she means now," someone says, but I don't know who, for it's just at this very moment we all realize Katie Ludwick is going to have a fucking baby.

We fire off a series of questions, mostly for our own benefit. She volleys back with primal screams and obscure curses. Adam and I run toward the bank, then stop. Dean yells, "She's got a big one!"

"Katie," Adam says. Then he says, "Hold on!" It's all he can think to say.

"Get out of the water," I yell. "We'll drive you to the hospital."

"This goddamn fish is not getting away!"

Still, she keeps taking slow steps toward shore, with something of a heightened sense of urgency. Dean's feet rise and fall in place. His skybound hands pull at the invisible taffy gumming us all to this moment in time.

"Is she seriously going into labor right now?" I ask.

"I think so."

"What do we do?" Adam says.

"Be a man," Amelia says.

"Come out, Katie. Drop the rod!"

Katie Ludwick spares two seconds to look over her shoulder. The death glare she gives me can only be interpreted to mean: *Go to hell or someplace similar. No baby is getting between me and my life. The baby can wait. You dudes can wait. Fuck off.*

Dean grins, guiding his sister to shore. Amelia says, "We need a blanket." I literally run around in circles. Everyone talks at the same time. How did we not bring a blanket? Dean, get over here. Take off your jacket, my jacket, Katie's jacket—lay it down there. No, right there. Katie you have to get out of the water!

With the boxing jacket spread out like an operating table, Amelia runs upstream to wash her hands. Adam empties the little ice chest and fills it with water. We stand there stupidly as Katie takes baby steps toward the shore, a reel here and a reel there. Her line getting shorter all the time. Dean moves toward us, gazing away at the hills, his arms stretched out to heaven. *Zozezaz.* When he lowers his arms, the breeze kicks in; when he raises them, the breeze dies down.

One Katie Ludwick foot comes out of the water and slaps down upon the shore. She demands Adam dump the water out of the ice chest so she can put her fish in it. Amelia tells him don't you dare! She's already unsnapping Katie's waders. I stand there not knowing what to do, watching Adam sort of crouch down and hunch forward like his body's trying to help in ways his brain hasn't figured out yet. Katie's eyes are on the water. Dean starts to laugh. Katie's rod trembles like a tuning fork. She grips it until her knuckles turn white. I see the fish's head dart out of the water and then dive. Katie lets a few inches of line slip through her fingers, then holds fast. Amelia's hands support Katie's armpits.

"Sit back slowly, there you go—Adam get up and help me—sit back on the jacket, Katie."

"I've got him," Katie says. "I've got this son of a bitch." She groans again. Her voice is a siren drowning out the roar of the river.

And then suddenly there's Dean, right in front of me. He's wrapped his hand around the spasming rod and is pushing it into my chest like a bouquet. I stare at him. "Take it," he says. I realize at that moment I have come home for this reason and no other. "Take it," Amelia says. I am not here to escape or to recharge or to reminisce. I am here to steady the rod so Katie can have her mystery baby without giving up her life, and for a moment my wandering legs become a source of stability.

Cradling a length of the pole in both arms, I catch the line when it slips. Dean turns away from us to face the crumbling pylons. I can feel the fish struggle and give in alternate beats. Katie's fingers barely cling to the rod's cork handle. The fish leaps again as if gasping for air. Katie's right leg still in the water as her body topples down the staircase of Amelia and Adam toward the jacket that serves as her blanket. For a second I am dazzled by the glare of the noonday sun as Dean seems to part the clouds, and the next thing I see is Katie's rod arc toward the river like the curve of the moon or a blind man kneeling down to pray.

Rome

Once you've sold it all or moved it into storage or burned it down with the house, once you've put the key in the ignition or bought the tickets or stuck out your thumb for the highway, once you've let it all go and found yourself in a strange countryside under the cautious eyes of inscrutable locals and told yourself that this is starting over, once you've started over, and then started over again...

She comes to mind less and less each day. Thinking about it doesn't hurt as much anymore.

I met another version of her in Rome, an Italian look alike. She wore the same glasses, had the same chin and the same eyes and the same love for wordplay.

Only I didn't know Italian and her English wasn't amazing, so it took a lot of explaining to make her get my stupid jokes. I had to ask three or four times, "What exactly is it that the Romans *do*?" I told her to drop me off outside the city just so that I could walk back in, turn around, point at the road and say it led me there.

We wandered all over the stratified city. She showed me the statue of Bruno and some zillion-year-old ruins that were taken over by stray cats. People walking by on their way from one coffee shop to the next, no longer concerned with the zillion-year-old history around them. I guess it's the same with me and wilderness. Is there anything we won't blur out over time?

Maybe they don't look so much alike. Her face becomes more and more difficult to picture each day, and my eyes haven't itched much lately.

I remember we found a boat moored on a sort of sidewalk under Hadrian's Bridge when the Tiber was low.

"We can live there," I said, not sure who I was talking to.

Once you've locked the door behind you, once you've forwarded your mail and found a place to stay for a few days until the weather clears up, once you've let everyone know you're coming and secured a few couches and found some temporary work...

Once you've said your last goodbyes and tried (and failed) to tell her the one thing you always held back

Once you've acknowledged you will always own this love no matter how much you sometimes wish you'd never met

Once you get on the bus and the world starts moving and the signs for new towns start coming into view

Once you reach a highway you've never seen before, surrounded by unfamiliar mountains or urban sprawl or flattened fields or mulish trees

Once you're no longer able to tell which way you're headed

Then you can lean back and listen to the bumps in the road, and try to read omens in the clouds. And you can pretend for a minute that you're finally going home.

ACKNOWLEDGEMENTS

Here's a book that never would have existed without Katie and Josh Ludwick, Jasmine Hopkins, Aaron Jennings, Kiva Singh, Alyssa English, Brad Wilson, Joel Vogt, Colin Westcott, Justin Merth, Ian Schoneman, and Josh Cudinski. And it wouldn't be in nearly the shape it's in if not for Sarah Jennings, Claire Mikeson, Joshua Hamilton, Shawn Mihalik, Brian Buckbee, Alyssa Rae Hands, and Coleman Pape.

I'm extremely grateful to Joshua Millburn, Ryan Nicodemus, Colin Wright, Marshall Hibbard, John Nilles, Jon Aaseng, Erika Fredrickson, Rebecca Schaffer, and Molly Laich for helping this book make its journey outside the Missoula city limits.

Some thanks whose connections I can't easily explain: Tatiana Allen, Rebecca Zuidervaart, Heather Miller, Eli Boland, Josh Ellis, Josh Merth, and Lauren Perry.

Thank you Butterfly Herbs, the Oxford, Flippers Casino, and the rest of Missoula. For being there when I needed you, and for not being there when I didn't.

ABOUT THE AUTHOR

JOSH WAGNER was born with a hole in his heart, a Ventricular Septal Defect (VSD). He's fine now. He studied Creative Writing at the University of Montana and received his MSc from Edinburgh University in 2019. Between all the schooling, Wagner worked occasionally in comics (*Fiction Clemens*), film (*Bleach Bone*) and theatre (*Salep & Silk, Ringing Out, Bleached Bones*), but prose remains his true and abiding love. His works of fiction include four novels (*Shapes the Sunlight Takes, Smashing Laptops, Deadwind Sea,* and *The Adventures of the Imagination of Periphery Stowe*) and dozens of short stories. He is interested in rhizomes, paradoxes, things left unsaid, and the ambiguities of longing and motivation. He spent his formative years by the ocean first, and then in the mountains. Torn between these forces, he can't sit still for very long. Wagner rarely lives anywhere for more than a year at a time, and his constant travels contribute to the particular imaginative flavor of his work. Yet he still hasn't mastered a single foreign language. Maybe someday.

OTHER WORKS BY JOSH WAGNER

Fiction

*The Adventures of the Imagination
of Periphery Stowe*

Deadwind Sea

Shapes the Sunlight Takes

Mystery Mark

plays and graphic novels

Fiction Clemens

Salep & Silk

Bleached Bones